The young hero, Abyss, continues on his quest to seal the chaotic God of Fire. However, the oddities that his magic has caused the world now throw him into a storm of misfortune. The boy must now deal with a crew of self-serving pirates, square off against the legendary hero Simon Williams, and crawl through the bizarre and deadly dungeon of the God of Fire.

The exiled and abandoned failures of heroes are led by the crafty and cynical Captain Friedrich Drake, who intends to harvest Abyss and cut him open alive. Escaping into a hectic coliseum, Abyss meets the spontaneous, mischievous Witch Dorothy, who seems to have many other odd plans for him in the back of her mind. However, the heroes and clerics alike have decided that Abyss has proven he's unfit for his original duties.

Waiting for the boy and his companions is a dungeon hidden in the stormy seas where the God of Fire resides. The dungeon holds herds of berserk chickens and octopuses, a deadly Field of Five Suns, and a disgruntled Child of Fire hiding the fated diamond blade. The final battles will require assistance from the immortal huntress Diana, and her hidden power, and demand an ominous sacrifice. With the ancient Pharaoh still yielding great expectations for Abyss and the legendary Witch he contracted with still hiding secrets, the darkest and deepest parts of his journey are yet to come.

Leaping Through the Fire

ISBN: 978-1-4874-4120-3
Cover art by Martine Jardin

Published by eXtasy Books Inc

Look for us online at:
www.eXtasybooks.com

Leaping Through the Fire
Journey into Chaos 2

By

Andy Hsieh

Dedication

For aspiring young heroes all over the world.

Chapter One

"Freeze something, anything to make a handhold!" I yelled as I felt dirt and small rocks scrape my entire left arm. Cold went through my right arm instead. "Don't freeze me, you idiot!" It was a miracle that I'd managed to slow our descent for so long.

"I'm trying!" Inder sobbed as she finally managed to touch the dirt cliffside with her hands and form a makeshift handhold. Our downward trajectory finally stopped as pain shot through my left fingers.

"Make . . . more . . ." My grip had already lost two fingers before Inder made another handhold for my right arm and leg. Now we had a little stepping stone around three inches long, and Inder took deep breaths.

She had to gather herself before creating the next few stepping stones.

"The cliffside slopes pretty gently if we just keep moving right," I said. I noticed that she was reluctant to use the stepping stones she'd created. "Uh, you could let go of me now?" I blushed, realizing that this was far more contact than I'd ever had with Diana.

"My ankle's sprained badly," Inder said. "I'm not that heavy, am I?" As she pressed against my back, I almost lost my grip while encountering a soft feeling. Diana was skinny enough to pass as a boy, while Inder was as well-endowed as any cartoon character.

"Once we get to stable ground, you can do some makeshift medicine, right?" I continued to use the makeshift handholds and footholds I was given until we reached the gentle slope. Once we sat down to rest, however, Inder was a bit too busy crying from the shock. And unfortunately for her, I really wasn't good in these situations. "Hey, things can't be that bad. With your magic, can't you shoot icicles and such if you practice hard enough?"

Inder shook her head. "It's really limited, I . . . I only had the dexterity to create an ice shield at most, since the crystals just automatically form." It was quite a sight to see her tears washing the dirt on her face. "But we're in the worst possible outcome now, especially since we're in the mutagenic fog. If you had been paired with Latis or Diana, we would definitely be able to survive."

"Well, since those two pack a great punch in combat, I'm sure that they'll survive and find us. As long as we conserve energy, find water, and build some sort of shelter . . ." My stomach rumbled to interrupt me and served as a reminder that I hadn't been able to finish that boar leg I'd been digging into. "And I'm glad I have you, right? Things usually go pretty badly when I have to fend for myself." I kind of expected Inder to go into some long backstory at this point.

"My fate has been sealed, no matter what universe I would be born into," Inder said. "As a child, I had always visited the hall of mirrors as a descendant of the Ice God. Most of it appears to be maintenance, like we're just janitors polishing the mirrors. But when we enter the hall, we see many different possibilities. Witches were supposed to originally save the world, but *save* always had different definitions. Humans were fond of inventing misery, and so . . . I'm pathetic, just playing the part, aren't I?"

I recalled the scenes I'd stumbled across with Simon in the quicksilver aether, where I had grown up to be a normal man, a fat comic book nerd, and a lonely, struggling artist and writer. "You can go on, even if . . . even if I can't understand."

If I was an utter klutz at saving damsels in distress, I wanted to at least be a good listener.

Inder shook her head. "As I said, whether it's comedy or tragedy, children of the Ice God have to play a part in one universe to the next, no matter how bad or incomplete the story is. That's . . . part of the secret of the universe, of the multiverse, rather. We're all stories within stories, continuing to pass between reality and fiction."

"So our purpose is as foreign as a body's well-being is to the individual cells that live inside?" I asked.

"That's not a bad analogy." Inder smiled. "My mother was a scientist, actually, and she worked hard every day to explain the mysteries of the universe. I always wished that I could follow in her footsteps, but when I was taken through the hall of mirrors, I could only admit that scientists made for rather boring storytelling. On the other hand, Latis' mother was just a cold-blooded assassin, and he's content with acting out his role as a knuckleheaded warrior."

"Well, I hope that you're only crazy or joking," I said. "I really don't want to imagine being the creation of some struggling writer living with his parents trying to find a profitable manuscript."

"In many cultures, gods, and fate play their roles accordingly," Inder suggested. "Maybe you can't become a god, a physical property of the universe. But if you could wrestle away their influence on this mortal plane, you could provide a more peaceful world."

"There's going to be chaos and misery regardless of scientific advancement or magical influences," I said. "Even if you think you're only cut out for a tragic death, Inder . . . I enjoyed the company you provided me till now. You're probably the only normal thing that an adventurer wants when he sets out on his journey." I turned away a bit and tried hard not to also develop feelings for Inder as puberty hung over my shoulder. "In any case, if you're good enough to walk, we should look for food and shelter. I'm not sure if we can find a way to signal to Diana and Latis, let alone find a way out of this thick fog."

I expected Inder to take the lead as she had more experience with the supernatural, but it appeared that she wanted to stick to the script she believed she'd been given. I tried my best to somehow summon the future-prediction snout that I'd managed when we'd fought the mutant boar, but I just looked like an idiot as I wrinkled my nose. Inder still limped as she walked, and she partially froze her leg to reduce the pain. When I looked around the fog-filled forest, I didn't find any more tracks of prey. I even lifted some rocks and rotting wood in an attempt to find insects and grubs. After a few failed attempts, I breathed a sigh of relief when I finally found a tarantula bigger than my hand.

"We can't be picky eaters here." I gestured to Inder to use her ice magic or any tools she could find, but she appeared to be as afraid of creepy crawlies as any teenage girl. "More for me then," I said as I reached out with my hand and grabbed the creature by the abdomen. Before I could even move it toward my mouth, however, blazing heat shot through my hand, forcing my grip open and giving the spider a chance to escape. I tried with my left hand with only food on my mind, but the tarantula swiftly darted away into the bushes and shadows, safe from my grip. "It beats being bowled over by a hippo, but . . ."

My right hand didn't show signs of bleeding or infection, but I doubted that the pain would go away anytime soon. I sighed as I continued to look around for edibles. "If my Diamorph abilities activate whenever I'm in danger, why don't I just adapt my stomach and teeth to make eating all this vegetation feasible?" Inder didn't seem to have the answer, so I went out on a limb and went for another round of trial and error. I stripped off some leaves from a nearby bush and popped them in my mouth. However, as soon as the plants hit my inner lips and teeth, I began to gag and cough up the two leaves, not even having an opportunity to chew them. "Is everything here . . . so disgusting to taste?"

"If we keep moving, we should be able to find some mushrooms," Inder suggested. "Latis never liked relying on them, but I hope you'll be a bit more open-minded."

"How bad can our . . . hallucinations get anyways?" I asked. "Will we end up fighting and killing each other?"

"I know how to reduce the poison enough with my magic," Inder said. "It'll just be like getting drunk. Although I'm not sure that you've experienced that either."

I came from a relatively uptight family, so I only ever saw adults get really drunk on TV and in movies. I knew that there was already a lot of talk among the eighth graders about trying out cannabis and it being harmless. But all the proper authority figures warned that anything could be the gateway drug when it came to substance abuse. None of them had ever advised for this situation. Heck, I hadn't even taken much survival training before meeting Diana. My stomach insisted that it would settle for anything I could put down my throat right now.

I tried to force myself to calm down as we trudged through the forest. "Some water will always bring you back to focus for a while." Inder was good at finding the underground network of roots and vines that carried water throughout this modified forest, so at least there was that. But the hours soon began to pass, and fatigue eventually began to set in. I tried multiple times to force some of the vegetation and tree bark down my throat, but all of the plants vehemently rejected my mouth. The sun was hidden by the shrouds of the forest canopy and fog, but I'd surmised that a full day had passed.

"I can sense the roots!" Inder exclaimed. "Mushrooms are

close!" She led the way toward the site of the edibles while she still limped a bit. My stomach growled violently in response. "It's a huge patch!" Inder gestured to the treasure of fungi growing on a collection of rotten logs. Most of them had brightly colored caps and patterns and were as big as my fist. I forced myself to wait as Inder reduced the toxins in the fungi with her ice magic and subconsciously forced a smile.

"Should we have a back-up plan just in case?" I asked as Inder took the first bite off a small mushroom. She didn't answer as she chewed, and I was hungry enough to throw caution to the wind as I scooped out a couple of colorful red-spotted ones and tossed them into my mouth, roots, dirt, and all. After waiting a few seconds, I only noticed that my stomach was giving off a contented sigh, and so I continued to shove the fungi down my throat. They tasted like any edible raw mushrooms, slightly bitter and crunchy, so far better than the raw eggs and grubs that I'd eaten with Diana at the beginning of my adventure.

I had felt like I'd cheated death enough and had gone through enough battles already, so I didn't feel like I could ever underestimate the power of fungi. Inder was probably still working on her third mushroom while I was working on my eighth, and she reached out for me clumsily. "Hang on, the spores here are spreading . . . wait for the dirt to settle a bit before plucking the neighboring ones . . ."

"I'm too hungry!" was all I could reply with. The effects of the mushrooms' toxicants didn't show until I'd already stripped more than half of the field clean, and I realized that my stomach still wasn't satisfied. When I reached for my next mushroom, it jumped up and babbled in a high pitch. I tried to chase after the mushroom, but in less than a second, it split into two, and then four, and then eight . . .

Dozens of big mushroom caps jumped up and punched me in the face in succession, and I forced my eyes closed as I stumbled backward. When I opened them again, everything was normal again. The field of mushrooms would have to try harder than that to stop me.

"Doesn't seem too bad . . ."

"Abyss, where did you get that kitten?" Inder said as I moved toward the mushrooms. Was she also hallucinating? "We're in class right now. Put your pets away. Now Stephen really doesn't let any counter-arguments for utilitarianism bother him. What do you have to say about that?" I tried to ignore Inder, but I was too woozy as I turned and stumbled to the side. Now I met Inder face-to-face, except . . .

Hssstt . . . Inder's head had been replaced with that of an anthropomorphic snake, and her forked tongue sniffed the air in front of her. "Smells like fresh meat, Abigail. Meat is when we leave Eden when apples spice up life, right?" I forced my eyes shut again, but things only got worse when I did so. Now I was completely stuck in my hallucination, and I came face-to-face with a zombie with green, rotting skin.

"Unfinished, sunshine . . ." the zombie boy hissed at me. "My only sunshine . . ." The zombie pulled out a sword that had been hidden in his skin and ran toward me. I was unarmed in this new hallucination, and I just needed to . . . open what? My eyes again, and maybe some water would do the trick . . .

"Eat up my little cuckoos!" Inder said as I was pressed into her soft bosom. I didn't have any time to push her away as her breasts became large fields of rolling cotton candy. And all of a sudden, I was swimming in this thick cloud as I tried to refocus. Taunting faces sprouted from the cotton fields as bits of them condensed to form thick globs of hungry, red meat. And from the endless pink clouds above, huge feminine legs rained down upon me, as if a group of teenage girls were daring each other to step on a scurrying rat.

"You can have her and many other lovely legs and their

glorious glutes!" It appeared that Oljatu was in this hallucination with me. "Spread strong sons and diligent daughters across the land like a proper khan!" It had to all be a hallucination, some . . .

"Dirt cheap comic relief? Heheheheheheh . . ." The voices of familiar cartoon characters rang through my head as I rolled around like a toddler in the endless fields of pink cotton. "Wawawa-wasure . . . washing an old person!"

"That's not fun!" I exclaimed as I ran forward and finally broke away from the cotton fields. I knew that I shouldn't leave Inder behind, but having her around only made my hallucinations worse.

"It is for me!" The voices were still there in my head. "Washing an old person. Washing old a person. Watching a person o-oh-old . . ."

"Abyss!" Inder exclaimed. "Come back here and . . ." the rest of her voice garbled again as the shadows of trees and foliage appeared through the pink and red flashes of delusion. Could I trust myself to make a perfect turnabout and find Inder? I could hardly walk straight without tripping over a thick root or so.

"Isn't it time I get a little break?" I was talking to myself as I rested my head against a tree trunk. My stomach hadn't been satisfied at all from the mushrooms, and I sunk down. I wanted more food, but how bad would the hallucinations get? "Sometimes the hero needs to act like a villain, right? To have those little gray areas isn't so bad if I'm just . . . another character in a story," I mused to myself. "What will I become then if I leave her behind?"

A few seconds passed, and I almost laughed to myself. I was reveling in my idiocy. "Those aren't hallucinations at all, right? Okay, some of them are." I stood up and tried to go back in the direction where Inder was. "I have to ask the Gods of Fire and Ice why they decided to take such interest in humanity. At the end of the day, aren't we just another by-product of physics? That even if chemicals create DNA and cells and life, deep down within the atomic structure, it's the same protons, neutrons, quarks, and such that mindlessly obey the rules of space-time?"

The fog was too thick for me to see in front of me, and there were too many tree trunks to try and compensate from my deviations. "Inder, are you there?!" I asked. There was no response.

This is a really bad way to go out.

I could only cross my fingers and hope that some animal would run in and see me as prey, and that would be enough for me to trigger the next evolution. A few minutes passed as I stumbled about nonsensically, and I felt my eyelids getting heavy. If I fell asleep while the mushrooms were still working their hallucinogens through me, would I ever wake up?

There was one last hallucination before I started to fade into unconsciousness. "Be defeated now, Abyss," a female voice spoke up. "Once you reach the Titan's Pit, you will serve your true function and be a true hero. Evil can be eradicated instead of fruitlessly fought if only . . ."

"If only . . ." I asked. "If only . . ."

For what seemed to be days, there was nothing but pain and shivers running through my body. I couldn't feel or move my arms or legs anymore, but I knew that my heart, lungs, and liver were breaking apart slowly while my intestines seemed to be tangling themselves and strangling themselves in a drunken rage. I had perhaps ingested dozens of different poisons by swallowing the mushrooms, and I was surprised that my body didn't immediately shut down. The hairs on my back turned into goose bumps—or rather, was my spine breaking through my skin and muscles and spreading its roots all through the universe like a voracious tree?

"Foolish, but quite durable," a deep male voice observed me. "The proper one to continue my legacy . . ."

"Aaaruahagh . . ." I could finally feel my vocal cords again, and I realized that the cacophony of sounds around me was finally becoming language. My eyes felt like they were stained with salt and acid. They rolled a few times in their sockets, the retinas finally reattached themselves, and my pupils began to focus. But even then, I wasn't quite *seeing*, but shared the memories of that ambitious and ruthless ancient Pharaoh.

Were they memories at all? Or was I looking into the future? A dark, distant realm between universes and worlds? There was a large, snake-like being ahead of us. Its scales branched out with many white and gray hairs and limbs, as it slowly carved its way through the sea of thousands of stars in the background. "There are so many precious things out there that must be preserved. But in the process, it's all being tragically compressed and warped, like diamonds in the rough," the Pharaoh continued. "All the pain, each and every fiber of your body suffers in order to carve out a better future."

"Fuu. Hrheehouu," I croaked, still unable to articulate my words.

"Humanity is limited, oh so limited. Think of all the other ways happiness, bliss itself might evolve," the Pharaoh explained. "That distant chain of *Becoming* you see carving its way through the universe will unify the best of all life, all sentience through the known universe."

And then, all of a sudden, I saw a future self—was that even me at that point? Scampering along the chain of *Becoming* on all fours while he balanced himself with a crystallized tail. Eagerly, he chipped away at the imperfections in the mystical chain. Or were they rather barnacles, parasites that were growing on a purer form of *being*? This was all so very confusing and perhaps would give philosophers of the past headaches and field days. But even with my doubts, I could feel the connection with my future self—actual, probably or possible and was amazed at his power, speed, and coordination while he ran on all fours. Even if he didn't take the upright form of a traditional superhero, he moved majestically and with a confidence that I envied.

"It might be thousands of years into the future from your point," the Pharaoh continued.

I didn't have complete control over my head or eyes, but somehow, I could see that further below and above my future self were other small figures, which carefully chipped away and polished the great chain of *Becoming*.

"At this stage, you have nothing but doubts, questions, and insecurities, but you play a vastly more important role in all of this than I ever will . . ."

What about Diana, Inder or Latis? What about the rest of the planet's eight billion people?

I wanted to ask, but my future self and I were beginning to strengthen their temporal syncing.

What mattered of the rest of the world when sheer bliss and beauty could not be contained in such social artifice?

The chain of *Becoming* captivated me once more, and upon closer inspection, its white scales were small, organized screens of millions of thoughts and experiences unlimited by the human kingdom. One moment I was soaring through the air, and then swimming through dark depths, crawling through mud and endless soil. And then there was the taste for power, lust to reproduce and multiply, flesh craving flesh stripping and consuming hundreds and thousands of tons of meat . . .

My eyes rolled painfully back in their sockets once more, and the Pharaoh seemed to sigh in disappointment. "The time will come one day, young Abyss."

All of the new experience, the truth, and actuality overwhelmed my human memories and limited cognition.

Something that had pierced the back of my skin was retreating back into my spine—my intestines and organs began to untangle themselves and revert to normal. And then came a deep, mechanical whirring as the scene suddenly faded from my mind . . .

I was floating in a long, large black screen in the midst of my dreams. All I knew was that my stomach was still hurting and that I hadn't eaten nearly enough. I was bouncing off long lines of what appeared to be computer code. Outside of this screen of code, a computer game was running, and beyond that screen was someone completely absorbed.

Game Over, the screen printed as I bounced around the lines of code. I was no longer a human body, even though I could feel my stomach, but perhaps one of the many software functions reading the long lines of code required to start the game. The player behind the screen hit *Continue*, and when everything began to reload, I saw that bits of pieces of the code around me turned into the colorful mushrooms that my body had just ingested.

"A computer can only be perfectly literal, but humans can be more. Is that a good thing?" I asked myself. Humans in the modern era had it easier than ever to submit their minds to an algorithm, if not through video games, then through internet filters. And even before there was any technology, stories would get told over and over and become a religion. I wanted to scoff at the God of Fire for giving humanity magical potential, if we were all just akin to trained lab rats, without a droplet of imagination for every ocean of habit and routine, of hedonism and comfort. For humans to become more like computers would perhaps be fitting.

The vastness of deep space and time could only welcome a species that rejected its biological body and sacrificed the arts for sciences. I was still stuck in this body and brain of mine, and I couldn't move.

How many days have passed since I'd consumed those

hallucinogenic mushrooms? Why hadn't some hungry animal just taken a bite out of me? Nature usually wasted no time . . .

I felt my jaw again and tried to shuffle it about like a lion would, even if there was no food, no hope, and no . . .

"He's stirring." I heard a female voice declare. I tasted barbecued meat, which I originally left to a happy hallucination, but I soon began to feel the back of my mouth, and then my throat . . .

"Not good. His jaw's going limp again, and we'll have to help him swallow."

Then I felt the entirety of my neck, and my lungs once again began to expand and contract as I took in precious air. Everything seemed so cold and bizarre, and even though the contractions were supposed to be automatic and natural, I felt as if I'd just attempted to sprint a marathon. The shock of it almost knocked me back into the odd dream again, or rather, fluid was still building up in my lungs.

"Start the chest compressions. His immune system dealt with the mushrooms' toxins surprisingly well, but it didn't work down his digestive tract."

Then I felt my chest muscles return as a jackhammer slammed into my ribs. And then frustrating numbness came over me again. Maybe it was the mushrooms, maybe it was me eating the mutant boar flesh while I'd just recently copied its form and function.

"His allies said that he needs food to heal, so I guess we'll feed him while trying to get him to expel the poison." I tasted more meat before there was another violent chest compression, and the odd cycle continued for at least an hour before I could manage to think somewhat clearly and feel my entire body. A burst of fluid escaped my lips as I finally felt my eyes roll in their sockets. Slowly, I remembered how to open my eyelids and first regained control of my arms. It felt like crystals were stabbing into each of my four limbs, and even if I had just been force-fed meat, my stomach was far from satisfied.

"Gah . . ." I mumbled and fumbled about for language.

"You're Abyss, aren't you?" A nurse with orange-chestnut hair greeted me as my vision came back to me. I had no proof that I wasn't still hallucinating, but I didn't feel woozy like I had been when I'd eaten the mushrooms. "The boy who made the contract with the legendary Witch."

"First time I've ever seen one shove so many mushrooms down his throat," another nurse commented. "But we've been out of work for a long, long time."

"Where's Inder?" I asked. "A blue-haired girl with . . ." I remembered her bosom turning into fields of cotton candy and meat, and shook off the thoughts for now. "With a sprained ankle. And Latis, and Diana, and . . ."

"Worry more about yourself, kid," the first nurse said to me. I looked around and found that crystals were indeed sprouting from my arms and legs and that bits and pieces of diamond were falling off of my body, as if I'd been encased in a series of hardened scales or chitin plating. "We were hardly able to pick you up without everyone on the ship trying to either kill you or steal your power. And once we picked you up, the God of Fire himself materialized us in the real world, deep along the stormy seas."

"Thanks for saving me, if I was just going to turn into a crystallized skeleton in the forest," I said. My stomach rumbled once more as I slipped my legs off the bed and attempted to stand. The diamond scales made it difficult to balance properly, but I was getting used to the pain by now, and perhaps I was also developing better balance. "But who are you anyway?"

"We're just servants of the troublesome Witch, Akarira," the nurse explained. "It's rather complicated, actually. In nature, animals rarely starve to death as there are always enough opportunistic predators in the ecosystem. But ever since agriculture and civilization developed, human beings granted themselves one of the worst possible ways to die. Whenever famine struck, human beings would be faced with the slow fate of starvation. Akarira wanted to pour all of her magic into making sure that human beings could avoid that worst possible fate . . ."

"And this all has to do with me pulling out the diamond blade again, doesn't it?" I asked.

"Ever since that occurrence, we've been able to perform our job like normal. We own multiple ships across the eddies in the Earth's aether field, but it will take a while for Akarira to manifest her mind and body on this specific one . . ."

As if on cue, the door opened, and in strolled a ghostly-looking girl wearing an apron. "He's awake after all! We'll stuff him up for the rest of his journey!" The girl wore her red hair in two buns and had mischievous purple eyes. She seemed a bit tired as she constantly winced and flinched. "Hi, I'm Akarira, and it's nice to meet the hungriest guest I've had since Harald."

"But where do you guys get all of your food?" I asked. "Do we really need these magical ships, or couldn't you just make food appear wherever people starve for more than a week?"

"The God of Fire is strange like that, isn't he?" Akarira replied. "In order to run this restaurant, I have to feel the pain of the meat and then use dozens of more of my bodies as fertilizer for the fruits, vegetables, and animal feed. He was impressed that I was able to handle being eaten by so many animals at once, but at the same time, he greatly restricted my services. Ach, these boars are chomping me up. But I've been a chef through many stories and universes, so if you've ever read your favorite children's book series where a couple of heroes magically get roast beef in Tartarus, there's a good chance that I was involved."

"So I can only eat until I'm full, then? But you guys will

appear whenever I begin to starve, won't you?" I asked. "Maybe I can get used to that . . ."

"I wouldn't recommend that," Akarira said. "Even with your Diamorph power, you wouldn't last very long in battle on an empty stomach, and you don't get to pick your battles either. But come over to the dining halls. Your friends have already eaten, unfortunately, and they're waiting for you outside. But many other starving wanderers here are eager to meet you."

I stumbled after the ghostly Witch and noticed that people of all shapes, sizes, and ages were having a merry feast in this magical restaurant. I didn't have a jacket or pants to conveniently hide my scars and diamond scales, and so the longer time I spent walking, the more attention I drew. Did I have any allies here at all? Luckily, there were a number of empty tables to choose from, and I sat down at one and realized that there wasn't a menu to choose from. Just as I began to think that I could survive this crowded environment if I kept to myself, a tall, handsome man with a beard walked over to sit across from me. He had brought his half-finished plate of food, as well.

I noticed that the golden armor he was wearing looked familiar and realized that he was one of Melosh's underlings or allies. The man noticed the concern in my eyes, and he tried to flash a friendly smile. "Just because you were chosen by a Witch doesn't mean we have to be enemies," he said. "There's no fighting in the Wandering Restaurant anyways."

"Aren't you just trying to trick me?" I wondered if I'd said too much already, and one of the waiters put forth three plates full of food. I dug in boorishly and used the food as a convenient excuse not to converse with the man. It was delicious enough to do so anyway, especially in comparison to my usual diet from the past week. Even if the steak wouldn't impress Gordon Ramsay, it wasn't hilariously overcooked and burnt like the prey I usually hunted down.

"You fought off Melosh just a couple of weeks ago, didn't you?" the man continued. I didn't reply, more interested in food than flattery. "I'm John Preston, one of the clerics that serve our savior."

"There is no savior," I said. "Just the two Gods of Fire and Ice, of the nonsensical patterns of order and chaos that the universe is eternally bound by."

"But you believe in something more than yourself, don't you? Even if your so-called friends are troubled by your foolish bravado and desperate attempts to play hero, I certainly see something more." John might've either been really good at acting or brainwashed—I certainly didn't know and hardly cared. "Haven't you wondered about the possibility that you might have a greater purpose, a savior?"

"People have wished for such things ever since they've painted animals on walls," I said. "But just as I particularly don't care about the tribal chants and customs of such cavemen, I can't see much reason to put faith in whatever prophet you claim to follow. Stories and art should be thoroughly enjoyed and appreciated as they are. It all goes downhill when people use them as demands for faith and obedience." I hoped that would be enough to shake off John's comments, but apparently, he insisted on continuing.

"There was a very talented cleric who would be willing to re-imagine every god that the cavemen believed in," John continued. "He'd probably even thoroughly archive every bad story that middle school kids would write. But not only is he powerful, but he's insane and unpredictable. So I pray for him, as I pray for you, as well. Both the desperate ones who want to believe in every god, and the ones that see nothing but skepticism."

I shoved a drumstick and some chopped potatoes down my throat before replying. "And what do you think? Is your god fair and able to transform into every sentient being, from an ant, to a boar, to a catfish, and grant them just desserts? Whether they were breathing their last breaths during the hunt or in a slaughterhouse, all animals want to meet their Maker . . ." I trailed off for a bit, but I cut John off before he could reply. "I saw it myself anyways, when I first fell into the oil field that all of these extinct species lived and died for no reason, and they're just using me as a desperate attempt to channel purpose . . ."

"The soul is simply something mysterious, young Abyss. It's something that cannot be seen with science or predicted with mathematics. I pray that one day you understand."

Perhaps now it was my turn to attempt to bargain. "Do the clerics have to be at war with the Witches and their heroes in the first place?" I asked. "What exactly convinces you guys that we're evil and need to be stopped?"

"Certainly, the meaningless chaos that you spread needs to be stopped," John answered. He announced his convictions without skipping a beat.

"Meaningless chaos?" I asked. "When you say that, it seems like you truly believe in a Garden of Eden rather than the forces of evolution that have lasted millions of years. That's all humans can be for now, right? Hedonists on the individual scale and then branches on the ever-expanding tree of life."

"Give up on him, Preston," one of the other clerics called from the other table. "All Witches and their heroes are too keen on suffering to receive the gift of faith." John appeared to ponder for a bit before he took his plate and moved back toward his group.

"Aye, don't blame me for trying, Jordan," John said as he looked at me one last time and sat down with the other clerics. I realized that I still wanted to ask Akarira more questions and delayed finishing my food before heading toward the kitchen quarters. I'd been too focused on feeding myself and getting this annoying cleric off my hands ever since I'd awoken.

"Faster on the potatoes! Keep a consistent size, with the carrots and broccoli as well!" The sounds of knives slapping against cutting boards and boiling water could be heard through the busy kitchen. Akarira was still commanding her fellow chefs, waiters, and waitresses, and she winced in her ghost form while she provided delicious and much-needed food.

"Hey, Akarira," I started. "I still haven't met the Witch that I contracted with. I'm not sure if it'd be for the best, but . . . I met a weird nature goddess that I also think was a Witch. Are all Witches this weird?"

"What's weird about me?" Akarira said. She tilted her head as she floated up to me. "You're the one erupting diamond scales and getting funky off of mushrooms."

"Well, it's not a contest," I said. "But you can't say you're happy with spending an eternity—or however long it will take for every last human to stop starving—in this bizarre charade of preparing food, right?"

"Humans are bizarre to begin with," Akarira replied. "They've always clung to myths and miracles before science, and even when you've made progress, most still prefer the bizarre." I scratched my head.

"Is that the reason why the God of Fire decided to bestow magic upon us?" I asked. "But . . . for me, even if I somehow return the diamond blade to its proper place, what's next? Will I have to do dozens of more weird quests before I die?"

"That's the way humans have always preferred it, right?" Akarira asked. "Any chef knows that no matter how delicious a meal may be, customers will still always want more variety, from spices to sugars and every kind of salt." Akarira had a point there. "It's not always the same meals I'm making, and it's not always the same animals I'm feeding with my body."

I remembered how badly my attempt to save Moka had gone and decided to let Akarira be for now.

"Although I'm sure you've heard this before, but you should be more worried about yourself. You ate a good bunch, but did you drink enough water? Because your body still has to flush out the toxins from the patch of fungi you consumed."

I did notice quite a bit of discomfort in my stomach, so I headed over to the counter and gathered a large cup of water from the fountain. Although this Moving Restaurant served beer and wine to the adults, it seemed to lack the modern luxuries of carbonated soft drinks. But I'd never been that much of a soda drinker and didn't want to risk complicating my healing process.

"If there's a restroom, where does it all flush to?" I asked. "Don't tell me that it all becomes efficient fertilizer for vegetables."

"If you're so curious, why don't you transform into a fish and swim down the drain?" Akarira asked.

I'd let my guard down because she saved me, but in the end, I had to remind myself that I couldn't trust every weirdo I met. And I wasn't sure what to say to Diana and Latis regarding my failure. It was always easy to imagine myself as the leader who suddenly developed confidence when I read comics and books, but in the real world . . .

My stomach rumbled as I finished another glass of water, which interrupted my train of thought.

How much of the mushrooms' effects had been mere hallucination, and how much was that peering into the hidden fabric of spacetime?

I headed over to the bathroom now, wondering if any of the hallucinogens would make their way through my bloodstream to my brain as they came out the other end. It was the first time in weeks that I was able to use a bathroom and toilet, but I couldn't be more grateful. A few months back, I'd eaten one too many spicy chips out of boredom, but this was at least ten times worse. It was as if half of my intestinal lining had been stripped away and forced to regenerate, and with every corrupted bit of organ tissue flowing through me, it scraped and chafed at my insides as it twisted and turned.

Just when I thought I was getting used to an adventurer's pain when it came to slugfests, I discovered something much worse. Hopefully, in the long run, I would either be able to develop some poison resistance from this experience or at least produce some useful chemicals after this. I wondered if Inder was okay on the outside and inside and realized that I couldn't simply shake off the mushrooms' hallucinations as easily as waking up from a dream. I was glad there was toilet paper and a sink to thoroughly wash my hands, and when my stomach continued to rumble, I wondered if I would have to repeat this procedure for multiple rounds.

When I returned to the dining halls, I was relieved to see a familiar face. Inder looked alive and well, but she had some gray bags under her eyes, as if she hadn't slept properly. "I'm glad to see you're still well, Abyss, but . . ." Inder began. "A lot of heroes and Witches have noticed the great distortions to space-time you cause every time you use your magic. They say that the only way to keep reality stable is to exile you from the world of magic after all, and they even set up a complicated spell."

"But then . . ." I'd wanted to take a small break as I started my second meal, but apparently, there was always bad news to hear. "Who will take up my quest to seal the God of Fire with the diamond blade?"

"That is yet to be determined from the spell," Inder said. "Quest Transfers between heroes are ultimately rare, but if the two heroes have a certain chemistry, it's possible. The God of Fire always welcomes unexpected developments, although the God of Ice wants comedies, tragedies, and epics to be set in stone from the beginning. And that's another thing about our quest. I didn't expect you to wolf down the mushrooms that quickly. Most people would need a break after three or four, but when you just chomped down on them and then ran across the forest, well . . . you did the devil's work and spread the spores."

"I'm guessing that made the fog worse and all?" I asked.

"Pretty much. We're still technically in the midst of the fog, even if we're out of the forest," Inder explained. "Surrounding us from all angles is a large body of water, and we can faintly detect the next island. In any case, even if you were to keep your quest, things wouldn't be pretty. Latis and I both spoke with our dad, and he said the best thing he could do to prevent the God of Fire from going ballistic is to seal him in a dungeon. And when we reach that dungeon, things won't be as smooth as in your . . . video games, or whatever you call them."

"Well, as long as you guys are all safe," I said. "The mushrooms didn't have that bad of an effect on you, did they?"

"Just some trouble sleeping and some nightmares," Inder admitted. "Try not to push your body too much after ingesting them, as even if you have advanced healing, you might risk breaking something."

"That's the only thing I've been able to do so far in this quest." I smiled grimly. I still hadn't told Inder about my own vision when I fell into the quicksilver aether when I viewed my possible future with Simon. "And . . . it's a whole lot more than I'd ever be able to do if I had been stuck on the mortal plane."

"Abyss," Inder said with earnest concern. "You're too good for settling for a hero's death." I knew that I should just take the compliment, but my frustration wasn't over.

"No, I'm really not," I said. "If the two of us were just . . . normal teenagers, eighth graders, heck, even if we shared four years of high school, I doubt that you would give me a second look."

Inder didn't push back on that statement—even if she retained her caring personality, she was far too attractive and would fit right into the group of popular cheerleaders.

"At least, not unless I was able to hit a sudden growth spurt and gain thirty pounds of muscle, right?"

"Maybe you won't change too much in shape and size, but try to believe that this is still just the beginning," Inder said.

"I've been pining for new beginnings ever since second grade, probably," I replied. "Maybe if I didn't have to transfer my quest, but if I could only switch my power, that would be good."

"Your power might be inconvenient, but it's also flexible," Inder said. "Latis, Diana, and I are all pretty limited as to what we can do."

I used the food in front of me to excuse myself from more conversation as Inder waited. After I finished my meal, I luckily didn't have to shed another lining of damaged intestine, and the two of us headed out of the Moving Restaurant. The building we were resting in was suspended in space-time by several pillars of quicksilver aether, and several docks extended out from this peaceful island. From what could be seen up ahead, the ocean was as violent as ever.

"It might take me quite a while to reincarnate if I die here," Diana said. "I've never sunk to the bottom of an ocean before, but if I was in a creek or a river, it would usually take much longer for me to grab the nearest human bodies and begin rebuilding." Diana didn't show any signs of worry on her face, as if she now expected me to survive bizarre situations. However, I could tell she was still frustrated at the fact that she had to tag along with the rest of us.

"Hey, look at the bright side," Latis said with a smile. "It's not every day that our quest lets us go and bust through one of Dad's dungeons."

"First, we have to get through all this water and the attempts to exile Abyss," Diana said. "As much as I want to work with a more experienced hero, he might be the only one with the power to seal the God of Fire."

"Hey, I'll get the hang of it all someday," I insisted. "If you have any tips to help me sprout the magical predictive snout again, I'm all for it."

"We can't afford for you to exhaust yourself on the way to your trial," Diana said. "Just stay put and help keep the ship stable when we set out."

Upon seeing our mode of transport, I was glad that it wasn't a small raft or a canoe, but it still wasn't anything to brag about. The ship was designed as if it had been ripped out of the Viking Age, with multiple mechanical modes of rowing replacing the tedious hand power.

"If we become stranded at sea, will the Moving Restaurant pick us up again, or will we have to eat each other?" I asked.

"Well, if that ever happens, you could make yourself useful and get us some fish until you drop," Latis said. "Although the God of Fire would wreak havoc on space-time long before we starve. Or he might let us starve anyways just to laugh at us."

"Why does this universe have to be so weird?" I asked as I got in the Viking ship and followed Inder's instructions on how to rig the enchanted machinery. "Why couldn't they just let me beat up Ares or Humbaba in a middle chapter so I could look cool for once?"

"Just focus on providing the power and cranking the gears," Diana suggested. "I'll take the vanguard and steer, and Inder and Latis will be on the lookout so we can avoid pirates."

Everything started smoothly, and luckily, I would be given maybe an hour or two of sanity since consuming the hallucinogenic mushrooms. Seasickness was slightly preferable to the shocks from riding Ibonus, and I let the waves create a rhythm as I provided the grunt work on rowing the oars. I was sure that we were taking quite a roundabout way to the nearest island, but avoiding fights and possible injuries sounded good to me. Life was probably both brutal and tedious for the majority of the ancient pirates and seafarers, and for a while, I thought about scurvy. Of course I was just waiting for things to go wrong by now, and as with every hero, things eventually did. The first few days of adventuring with Diana seemed so peaceful in comparison.

"The air . . . it's different all of a sudden," I said, and I noticed flashing bright and dim spots as if pockets of wind were expanding and contracting.

"Maybe you caught a farting dolphin or something," Latis jested, but Diana confirmed my suspicions.

"Crud, maybe all of our steering was for naught," Diana commented. "But for them to appear this quickly, that would mean that . . . *she's* involved, too!"

Before I could ask Diana who she was talking about, three large pirate ships surrounded us. They had manifested from thin air as they spun on water. Inder stepped in front to guard me with an ice shield, but she was quickly blasted aside by a powerful jet of water. Now I had two men twice my size backing me against the mechanical propellers, with the enchanted water right behind threatening to turn me into a *Happy Meal* for a lucky school of fish. Still, the water had been generous in giving me mutation before, and if I made any sudden movements on our small boat, it would probably put my three allies at risk.

"I'll catch up with you guys later!" I yelled as I jumped overboard head-first into the cold, dark waters. My entire body went numb from the shock for a split second, and I quickly forced a Diamorph transformation. I felt scales and fins begin to erupt on my legs. I would have to stay underwater until I was far out of sight . . .

"A fresh catch!" one of the pirates exclaimed. A powerful, rough cord tore into my muscles and bones and tore off the shroud of water above to expose me to air. I'd jumped right into a large fishing net, and my opponents had easily predicted my move. I was now on one of the pirate ships, and I was shivering and gasping for air. "See, Marvin, I told you he'd jump right in. And looks like the stories were true after all. He can erupt body parts from all over the animal kingdom!"

My fins were now useless—now all I needed were teeth and claws, anything to break free from the net, but as I had been warned, my Diamorph transformations were limited.

"Abyss!" Inder called from our boat, well blocked off by the two other pirate ships that had surrounded us.

Crap, what can I do now? Hope that the pirates don't eat me and dance in their circus show until I find a way to escape?

I noticed that around half of the pirates on the ship that I was on were puking out the remains of their breakfast and lunch, leaning over the edge of the canoes and shivering. "Teleportation magic isn't so kind to us fallen heroes. But it looks like we have plenty of crystal left for the future, huh?"

If I couldn't fight, I had to quickly look for hints and talk my way out of it. "For such a powerful Witch, Dorothy sure leaves her prized possessions in poor security."

"Well, she's got a bit too much power on her hands anyways," another one of the pirates spoke up. "I just wish the Witches would live up to their names and stop rooting for such goody-two-shoes. The world could always use a few more shades of gray."

"But about the boy, Captain. Do you still think we can capitalize on his power?"

"Water can draw the secrets from everything," the captain spoke. "As rivers twist and wind and shift and bend, we, the fallen heroes, will once again have their day. But first, let us inspect the boy, shall we? I'm Captain Friedrich Drake, one of the greatest heroes to ever abandon his quest. And now one of the greatest pirates riding the mutagenic seas, slaying monsters and men alike."

I still hadn't sharpened up on any of my lying skills, so I decided to tell the truth. "I'm Abyss, and you're interrupting a pretty important quest. If I don't seal the God of Fire, something very bad will happen to the world . . ."

"Bad for who?" Captain Drake responded with his sharp tongue. "It can only be good for us exiled heroes if the God of Fire is loose. Then we'll finally be able to break away from these stormy seas we were forever condemned to. In fact, why don't you ask yourself why you're so blindly following orders from these quest-givers?"

My bottom half was as tired and weak as a fish out of water. "Well, as weird and troubling as my quests will get, I'd certainly rather live a life of a hero rather than a pirate like you," I said. Drake was both amused and disappointed with my response. "I didn't get the perfect friends and companions like most adventurers could hope to wish for, but I still care for them."

"Ah, so you're as young as you appear, huh?" Drake responded. "To still be at that age when you believe in friendships, and not having yet learned to properly take responsibility for yourself. It might take many years for us to hone you, and by then, the world might change too much. Very well." Drake turned to his men. "Once we reach the Surgeon's Island, we'll vivisect him and see what powers we can harvest from him."

"Vivi . . . you want to cut me open *alive*?" I asked.

"Oh, don't be so mortified," Drake said with a smile that revealed a row of crooked and rotting teeth. "Humans have used tens of hundreds of thousands of animals for the sake of advancing science. Surely you don't think yourself so highly as to not be another piece of the puzzle for progress?"

"Even if I can transform my body, my mind is human enough," I said, trying to be assertive. But was that really true? I had fallen into quite a few hallucinations and odd dreams ever since I left the Western Sanctuary. I tried to thrash with my scaly legs once more and attempted to create sharp talons, but the action only resulted in another failure.

Drake looked down at my transformed legs with another smile before he summoned his water magic, created a small blob around the size of a baseball, and rubbed it across my skin. "You're more bizarre than any hero, and I've seen my fair share of strange things. But maybe we can keep most of you alive after we harvest your four limbs and have you serve as a jester."

"Let's not take too many risks with him," another pirate spoke up. "Even if it's a rarity, some animals, like starfishes and axolotls can regenerate. If we want to keep him alive for future use, we should keep him at the Surgeon's Island."

"Oh, Marvin, when will you learn to develop a sense of humor?" Drake asked with a smile. "Come, let's have him humor us some more. Just make sure nothing gets between us and the hospital. Even if we drove out those two brats from the Ice God and that four-millennia-old huntress, there are countless others who might want his head."

I stopped and paused for a bit and thought of strategies. "Are you guys stuck in these stormy seas forever? Is there any way that you could redeem yourself, or . . ."

"Nothing's impossible for the two gods, but they're content to let failed heroes either ride it out here or perform work in the Titan's Pit," Drake answered quickly. "We've heard many rumors that you were chosen by the legendary Witch, the ace for humanity's salvation. Only because you happened to be at the right place at the right time, sacrificing yourself to save a child, right? But if she actually was able to judge us all fairly, we would also be given another chance. But all of us have long lost faith in the Witches." Drake took out a bottle of liquor from his coat and took a big swig, which seemed to numb some of his memories. "But in a sense, our fate isn't that different from that of most adults. For the sake of efficiency, every generation allows itself to fall into mindless routines as they age. Tell me then, youth, why do you seek to be a hero?"

"It's just . . ." I remembered talking to John in the Moving Restaurant. "It's just like in any adventure story, even if real life is never like that. I want things to be exciting and weird enough, and I want to be lucky enough to make the world a better place, little by little."

"What world?" Drake asked. "The human world? If you can already become part fish or part cetacean, why not commune with the whales and dolphins and help them hunt and fight?"

"With the way humans hunt them down, he'd have to do a whole lot of repopulating," another pirate spoke up, and Drake slapped him across the face with a watery tentacle. "Or maybe he could transform into an octopus if he wanted to get real funky, or a cuttlefish." Still, some of the pirates laughed, apparently bored enough to entertain such jokes.

"It's just rough instinct, sure," I said. "And maybe if I somehow escape from you, I'll make mistakes in my judgment. But I'm satisfied with trusting human altruism, whether its imperfections come from evolution or poor individual development."

"And the lot of us pirates are satisfied with trusting, planning, and profit," Drake said.

I was hoping I could bargain a little more, but Drake left me in the net to help assist his men with other tasks. Two of his underlings had been assigned to look over me, but they didn't show half the amount of interest as their captain did.

Slowly, my fins and scales began to revert back into normal human legs, but it was little comfort as my powers and abilities remained limited.

My stomach turned at the thought of vivisection. I'd gotten through most of my other problems alive through sheer luck, but my encounter with the hallucinogenic mushrooms had almost put me in a near-death situation. What if help arrived to me when I had already lost an arm and a leg? Then I could be an actual pirate with a hook and peg leg, right? I chuckled grimly to myself and hoped that I could at least keep two of my biological limbs, and if not, I would be given an awesome cyborg suit.

"The seas are too calm around here," one of the navigators on the other side of the ship declared. "It couldn't possibly be . . ."

"We're already docking onto the island," Drake decided. "Just stay ready for battle, and we should be able to kill two birds with one stone."

Great, something weird was happening. Maybe I could get away with only losing a finger or two.

The captain returned to help escort me to the Surgeon's Island, and had two men at each of his sides. I wondered if I could talk myself out now. "Are you guys really willing to lose half of your crew to whatever surprise attack just to steal some of my power?"

"We're pirates. We live and die for power," Drake answered. "Entire generations have died for less, whether in work or combat."

"Here he comes," one of Drake's henchmen announced. Immediately Drake's more powerful underlings had sunglasses and visors up, while his lower-ranked men quickly fell one by one to a blur of gold and red. There were quick fragments of images, as if a video was playing on a slow computer. An agile knight in golden armor was wielding a crimson sword and quickly fought for a second before he disappeared into a burst of light. What quick glimpses I got of him, I could find that he had messy blond hair and a mad, bewildered look on his face.

"Whoever can subdue him will be promoted to my right-hand man," Drake announced. The golden knight took a bit longer to deal with the stronger pirates, as they wouldn't be stunned so easily by the flashes of light he could summon. Still, his swordsmanship and footwork, combined with the whip-like reach of the crimson blade he wielded, eventually made it so that the only ones still standing were him and the captain himself. Drake finally let go of me as I dropped to the ground in the net, but not before he pinned my lower half to the ground with a blob of highly pressurized water.

"The light does not waver," the golden knight declared with a smile. Upon closer inspection, much of his armor seemed like he was one of the clerics working alongside Melosh, but I noticed many different etches and patterns. "Even to the darkest depths of the ocean, it pierces . . ."

Captain Drake smiled in return. "Your swordsmanship has improved, but dispelling your blood arts still comes easy to me." Drake snapped his fingers and broke apart the knight's crimson sword, which apparently was woven out of liquid blood. "Of course, you don't plan to duel with me after all, am I correct? You're only here to get the boy. I thought you stopped doing the bidding of the clerics years ago, Xavrnos, the Unshaded."

"But he doesn't quite belong on the vivisection table. At least bring him to a sacrificial altar," Xavrnos insisted.

"And as mad as always," Drake said. "Even if you take him out of my hands, Unshaded, he won't escape here in one piece . . ." The pressurized water that trapped my legs now dug into my abdomen and felt around for the most useful organ to steal. "I'm no doctor, but I've stolen quite a few organs."

I bit down the pain and concentrated on Xavrnos. *What was he waiting for?*

Swirling light was gathering around his ankles and feet. I really hoped that he wouldn't spend twenty minutes charging something up while going on a tangent and detailing his backstory.

"One day, I shall be like light," Xavrnos declared. "And your little water magic will be nothing, a small change in refractive angle as I pierce through you."

With that, the Unshaded made his move, and I felt a nasty rip erupt within my organs.

The next thing I knew, I was speeding along the stormy seas in a small motorboat equipped with machinery that could run on Xavrnos' light magic when he ran out of fuel. I was losing blood quickly, even if I still felt most of my body parts intact. Drake had apparently been more meticulous than a butcher, as he wanted to steal my body parts in one piece.

"Won't he just come after us again with the teleportation crystal?" I asked.

"Not in another twelve hours, at least," Xavrnos answered. "It takes time for the magical artifact to cool down. As long as you're out of the stormy seas . . . or out of the magical world entirely by that time . . . he won't be able to pursue." Xavrnos quickly rummaged around for the ship for jars of medicine, apparently having prepared for this situation.

"Thanks for . . . wait, what is that?" Once Xavrnos opened up the jar, I noticed it appeared to be a carefully preserved tumor rather than any helpful sort of medicine. "Does that even match my blood type?"

"You'll receive more refined healing once you reach the coliseum," Xavrnos answered as he slapped the tumor onto my open wound, quickly stitching up the new flesh with his blood arts. "We have to stop the bleeding, right?"

I groaned and almost peed myself from the pressure and had a better idea of what had been harvested. "But I still have to fight whoever's trying to take my quest from me with . . ." I rubbed at my rib cage and gritted my teeth from the pain. "Without a kidney, I guess, and missing a couple of ribs. If I eat something, will they grow back quickly?" I cut myself off as I made a quick declaration. "But I'm not going to eat one of your preserved tumors, no matter what you insist."

"Hasty as always, just like any young hero," Xavrnos said. "First, there has to be the proper gatherings and arbitration before jumping into battle."

"Thanks for saving me anyway," I said. "But you were joking when saying that I'd be put on a sacrificial altar, right?"

"You wouldn't look bad on it," Xavrnos responded with a toothy smile. Observing his bulging, wrinkled eyes, the cleric seemed half-sane at best, as if he'd been driven mad by a combination of desperate prayers and grotesque imagery. "But before that can happen, even I have to get Dorothy's approval when it comes to dealing with you. I was hoping that your patron Witch herself would show, but for the sake of some sanity, perhaps I'll have to settle. Ohohoho!" The Unshaded chortled to himself. Even out of battle, something wasn't quite right with this guy's mind.

Chapter Two

The coliseum appeared as if it had just been duplicated from the remnants of ancient Rome, but oddly enough, there wasn't a surrounding village. Xavrnos the Unshaded apparently elected to stay on the small motorboat as I walked onto the docks, for better or for worse.

"I'd stay and watch, but both the Witches and the gathering crowd here don't take too kindly to me . . . at least, not yet." The golden knight once again flashed his mad smile before he turned around his motorboat and sped off.

I wasn't sure where exactly the main entrance to the coliseum was, but after a few minutes on the barren wasteland, I saw a familiar face and gulped.

"So it looks like you got lucky. We all got lucky," Simon Williams said. He still towered over me with his muscular frame and well-kept beard. Simon's appearance reminded me that even though I had grown more powerful in the last two weeks, I hadn't grown an inch taller. "It would have been pretty bad if those pirates got their hands on you."

"You're behind this whole Quest Transfer idea, aren't you?" I asked.

Simon shrugged. "A lot of us thought an early death would be the best for you, as it would resolve our problems quickly. But now that you've gotten this far while still fumbling about clumsily, we're worried what the future may bring."

"Well, everyone starts out clumsy, don't they?" I asked. "If this is about me eating the mushrooms, I'm pretty sure the Moving Restaurant gave me enough food to work it through the other end . . ."

"Follow me." Simon turned as he led the way toward the coliseum. I remembered all the betrayals and double agents I'd seen in fantasy stories and comic books. Still, I didn't know where to start if I had to outsmart Simon, let alone fight him.

"Don't you think that . . . well, destiny chose me for a reason?" I asked. I knew how lame I sounded, and Simon seemed unsure how to answer that idea.

"I've cleaned up many messes, and almost every hero I had to deal with was stubborn as a mule when it came to the Quest Transfer." Simon sighed. "But my patron Witch insisted that she wanted to meet you before the official transfer." As Simon neared the gates of the coliseum, I saw another familiar face I didn't want to see—Justin, the boy who could create pacts and seals with his words. But it was hard to stay mad at him because he was covered from head to toe with bruises and bandages. "Just create a clearing for us to discuss," Simon said as he turned to Justin. "Everyone in the coliseum wants blood, and many even bet for Abyss to make an upset. But if he makes the willing choice, we can do it the easy way."

Justin nodded and began to mutter an incantation under his breath. I thought over my words, and Justin stopped mid-chant. "No deception here, abysmal boy."

"What about Sonny, or Ruth, or the other people from the Sanctuary?" I wanted to get another person on my side.

"If you can't even plead your case independently, you're not true hero material," Simon said.

I chuckled and took the bait. "We both saw the vision in the aether after I defeated Grigory, right?" I asked. "I didn't have any spectacular fate if I returned to my normal life. It might not be a bad life compared to those of peasants, soldiers, and slaves throughout history, but . . . I'll get better day by day, week by week, and even if it takes years, this is my best shot at making the world a better place. I don't want to leave Diana and Inder, or even Latis, behind. Surely you two wanted to run away before but felt the same, didn't you?"

Simon shook his head. "Nothing is ever set in stone, Abyss. If you returned to your life, it might be true that you'd never be a genius inventor or a basketball star, but small acts of kindness and inspiration create ripple effects. The Gods of Fire and Ice that rule over the universe don't need particular heroes to step up . . ."

"What are you then?" I asked Simon. "After taking over so many heroes' quests, isn't it also your time to retire?"

"Who knows what I've become?" Simon asked, to my surprise. "When you saw my power for the first time, it was just the tip of the iceberg of my patron Witch's power. More than just teleporting through space, things like quests, destinies, memories, and periods of time are all within my reach. Everyone wants to be the hero of their own story, and there was a time when I had that type of mindset, too. They say that two heads are better than one, and if that's true, perhaps it's only a matter of time until there are enough Quest Transfers for me . . . for us to elevate to higher status in the eyes of the Gods of Fire and Ice, and allow our species to progress."

"Who's *us*? What species to evolve to?" I bemused. "Even if I'd just walk away empty-handed, I'd rather face the God of Fire myself in this quest rather than become a lab rat for your experiment." As those words left my mouth, the tumor that Xavrnos had installed in my wound flared up, and I again fell into the pit of oil that I'd experienced after the fight with Bethany. More and more animals were eating me in an endless chain of flesh and digestion, as if their lust for combat had awakened after coming face-to-face with this handsome exemplar of heroism.

"You'd best ask yourself that question," Simon said. "Is it worth it just for your curiosity? If you leave your quest to me, your friends will move on from you quickly enough, and you'll still have sound mind and body till your waning years. With every new power and transformation that you've gained, you put another level of stress on your brain and body."

Something in the tumor that had been installed turned inside out, and I no longer felt the endless rows of teeth shearing away at my flesh. "But isn't that the point of living then?" I smiled as I bit down the pain. I could see that Justin wanted to roll his eyes. "If, in the real world, I couldn't put my all in a sports stadium or in a research lab, so then I can only do this . . . special, weird thing that heroes do on adventures."

Justin's incantation grew more rapid and stressed until he finally choked and keeled over, and I looked around nervously preparing for the next obstacle.

"With every new Quest Transfer, Simon becomes more hero-like, but also more of a buzzkill," a bubbly female voice said. "But at least he always puts up a good fight, and in the end, that's enough, right?"

"You have until tomorrow to reconsider," Simon said as a broom suddenly appeared in his hands. Justin looked annoyed that he'd used up all his magic for nothing but didn't show resentment at the tall redhead. "When you meet my patron Witch, Abyss, don't listen too carefully to her. She'd let you explode into fish food if it meant making her laugh for a few seconds."

As I wondered how to respond to Simon's warning, the world around me went black. The next thing I knew, I opened my eyelids and was resting on a pillow. I couldn't feel my arms or legs, and the best I could do was twitch my ears. When I was turned by my jaws so that I was face-to-face with a beautiful pink-haired Witch, I finally realized the insanity of my situation.

"My body's gone, isn't it?" I groaned. "How am I even making noise?"

"So your body doesn't panic if it's my magic, huh?" The Witch had her hair tied up in twin braids, dressed in mostly black with white frills, and had a curvy body—it was hard to estimate, but with her long legs, she appeared to be slightly taller than Inder. "Now I really wonder what Grime-girl is made up of. But alas, the contractual magic says that we have to keep everything under secret. *Bleh*!"

"Can I just have my body back now?" I asked. "Or is this practice so that my head can fly around disembodied as a way to fight against Simon?"

"Hmph," the Witch said as she snapped her fingers. As my body popped back into place, I fell to the ground awkwardly as nerves and blood vessels coursed through my arms and legs. "I suppose it's good for you to keep your overall sanity like this. To not meddle too much with space-time despite her true power. But where are my manners? I'm Dorothy, one of the greatest Witches to ever walk the Earth."

"Did you let those pirates give me trouble, as well?" I asked. "And I thought . . . you were supposed to kill the Witch with a bucket of water, right?" I scratched my head. "Or is Toto now one of your angry minions you can summon to fight . . ."

"I'm like Simon without the boring of it all!" Dorothy said as she clapped me across the shoulder. "If I could, I would keep changing my name, but they say it's the remnant of my sanity to house at least one name. Well, that and Simon is the one that holds my sanity together, even though I provide him the power. But it doesn't always have to be him, right? If you pull the upset and take the Quest Transfer, I can be another . . . one of those . . . side quests, right? Like in books and video games, additional lore is always welcome, welcome!" Upon the last word, Dorothy broke into a sing-song voice and twirled about while she danced toward the nearby table and umbrella. A teapot and cup were ready.

"If you aren't lying about being one of the greatest Witches," I started as I sat down across Dorothy and carefully examined the tea she poured. "Is my patron Witch as . . . insane as you are?" I asked.

"Probably more insane, but also more serious?" Dorothy asked. "She's a delicate girl who takes her job too seriously, if I recall. But in a sense, I'm more generous, right? If I'm teleporting everything, from space-time to memories, at least I guarantee a fresh start, a new story, and spice. She's the sort of person who could be as exact as a computer program, who could make her hero die dozens of times if it was to produce the right outcome. But . . . I'm not to interfere too much or tell you too much, right?" Dorothy had apparently decided that the tea was too bland by itself and summoned some macaroons and other pastries. "Oh, don't be so hesitant! Eat up, as you have plenty of growing to do."

"You should know Simon best," I said, recalling how one-sided my first fight against him had gone. "Even if I had more speed and power, it's still hard to fight him if he can teleport right and left. Do you know how his patterns go?"

Dorothy looked at me curiously as if I was a fourth-grader trying to conceal cheating on a math quiz. "Perhaps Simon is right if all you want is to discuss patterns. If he wins the bet and you go back to normal life, you can learn tons of patterns in code and video games!" I gulped and almost choked on the sweet pastries. "You were able to replicate the boar's future sight in the mutagenic fog, were you not?"

"That's right," I said. "But if I can even do that, in addition to manifesting animal parts and creating hardened diamond plates . . . is it really possible that I can steal Simon's powers if the fight goes on long enough?" Dorothy didn't seem to want to answer such predictable questions, and so I shrugged. "Maybe if you give me one of your eyes . . ."

"What you really need is a better replacement than what

that mad priest-warrior gave you," Dorothy said as she walked over to me and inspected my abdomen. "You've got to take better care of your organs. You said that you were attacked by pirates?"

"Someone by the name of Friedrich Drake, I believe," I said.

"If it was the real Drake, then odds are you aren't getting your stolen body parts back," Dorothy said. "But luckily, I can rummage through my collection and get you something better than a preserved tumor." Dorothy reached into her robes and pulled out a couple of rings from under her breasts. "I'd feel bad if I was really replacing your kidney, but with this, I'll also be able to keep an eye on you."

"Aren't you . . . mostly disappointed me how boring I am, asking all these normal questions?" I asked.

"Right now, I am, but I see potential," Dorothy said. "Especially with your power." The Witch leaned over and unexpectedly stroked my cheek with her slender fingers. "The worst thing about becoming so powerful is not being able to be . . . surprised, enchanted again by mortal men and their offers." I felt Dorothy work her magic, and immediately, the awkward lump in my abdomen faded away. "I would settle down with another Witch, but alas, twist them like the dolls they are, and they begin to beg and groan."

"Thanks for fixing my missing kidney, but I'm really not . . ." I began nervously.

Whiz!

As Dorothy pulled away from my cheek, a spinning arrow whirled about on her fingertips. I could see that a trickle of blood was running down her index finger, as if she'd struggled to catch the projectile and pull it into a harmless spin. "You're still quite the shot as always, aren't you, Diana?"

"Abyss has already gone through a lot of weird stuff without you butting in, Dorothy," Diana said as she stepped into the tea party. Even though she held up her usual frustrated façade, this time, I knew she was hiding something.

"Ah, I . . ." I started. "Sorry, I got myself kidnapped by pirates," I said. "Hopefully, I'll just be more prepared the next time. Unless you just plan on telling me to concede my quest to Simon, huh?"

"I don't have any grand plans for you like Dorothy does," Diana began. "But I've decided to see that you finish this quest at least." It was a surprise to hear that, and the cheetah-cheeked hunter appeared to be concealing a blush. "For centuries, I've let life go by while not expecting much from heroes, but . . . if you were able to beat Grigory and deal with that mutagenic boar, I'm eager to see what's in store for your future."

"Let loose with your feelings for once," Dorothy smiled. "Indeed, humans have too often waited for heroes and priests to save them. If you can inspire even one out of ten you meet and add some color to the gray world, you'd do the job that any hero needs to do."

I remembered how I'd just rushed in to save the girl on impulse and continued to risk annoying Dorothy. "Why did you choose Simon to contract with as your hero?" I asked.

"Did I choose him, or did he choose me?" Dorothy asked. "When much teleportation magic comes and goes around, causality and memory all tend to get mixed up. If all you have are questions, though, young Abyss, you're going to end up with more questions than answers." Dorothy swiped her hands a bit and summoned more pastries and sweets. Diana shook her head and took me by the arm.

"Don't eat too many sweets," she advised. "Even if it's not literally poison, it'll weaken your chances when you square off against Simon tomorrow morning." I looked back at Dorothy and wondered if she maintained her figure by teleporting away excess fat.

"Well, you find any tasty grubs for tonight?" I jested. I had eaten a good share at the Moving Restaurant, but since I'd spent quite a few hours on the stormy seas with Captain Drake and the mad Xavrnos, I would sleep better if I refilled my stomach.

"We probably won't be able to afford anything you'd conventionally eat, but whenever a Quest Transfer happens, and clerics and heroes gather, there are always local hunters and chefs ready to serve the audience," Diana replied.

"Are there that many people really eager to watch a tall redhead and a short kid square off?" I asked. "I still don't get why Simon thinks it's his job to clean up my quest. I mean, aside from Moka, I didn't do that badly, right?"

Diana shrugged. "I've never pledged my fealty to the heroes and Witches, so I haven't bothered to really understand them." As we walked outside of Dorothy's private room and went through the coliseum halls, men and women began to take notice. I didn't think there was anything distinct about my appearance, but there were probably dozens of ways to sense who I was.

"So he's as short as they say, isn't he? Are you really betting on him, Carl?"

"Gotta love an underdog," Carl seemed to respond. Most of the observers concurred that I would have a tough time defeating Simon being outmatched in both experience and ability. Finally, Diana made it to the food stall, where the main choice of cheap food appeared to be oysters, clams, and cephalopods harvested from the surrounding seas.

Diana took out one of her knives and chopped up some writhing tentacles into smaller bits. If I could eat a grub, I could definitely try some questionable calamari, but it wasn't disgust that was holding me back. Diana put the chopped tentacles in a pan and roasted it over an open fire. "Is it really time to experiment with new techniques?" I noticed that others were staring at me, and Diana sighed. My cheeks and forehead both felt like they were sprouting extra bone and muscle, just like an octopus did when it blended in with the environment.

"Well, er . . ." My tongue felt long, as if it was turning into a tentacle, and Diana pinched my cheek hard. I winced for a bit, and when I opened my eyes, she appeared relieved.

"Trying to use octopus power won't help you in the fight with Simon, but it'll come in handy someday." My stomach rumbled, and I stomped my feet a bit to remind myself that my bones were still in place.

"Amateurs!" one chef exclaimed, berating his assistant. I turned to see that a skinny youth was trying to wrestle an octopus to the table. "Distracted so easily! You didn't even add nearly enough salt!" The head chef took a large handful of salt and smashed it into the head of the writhing octopus to prevent its escape. A second handful was poured on, and I winced as I imagined the pain the creature was feeling. The chef sliced off the tip of the octopus' tentacle and popped it into his mouth. "We'll give him out for free, but the taste has been ruined."

"Can't be any worse than the grubs," Diana said as she popped another cooked tentacle into her mouth. "Our budget and trade options are limited to what Latis and Inder carry, so make use of the free food."

As I walked toward the chef, I noticed he'd finally put the octopus out of its misery after immobilizing it, stabbing it through the head. "Spice it up, Markov's way," the chef said to his lackey. "Even a poor kid scrounging about doesn't deserve the octopus' true flavor." The skinny assistant nodded nervously and poured spices over the dead creature. The tentacles were still writhing aimlessly, and unlike the grubs, dozens of suckers were eager to choke me on the way down.

"So I guess I might see what Squidward tastes like," I said as the assistant began chopping up the dead carcass. At least his knife skills weren't bad. As I received a full plate of tentacles and headed toward Diana, I borrowed a knife and made sure to make the writhing bits as small as possible.

Diana noticed that I was hesitating. "Do you relate to these guys because they're intelligent?" she asked. "It's not like they'll return the favor if you try to save them, you know."

"I wonder which species would be the quickest to enact revenge on humans, though," I replied. "Pigs and octopuses are both smart, but pigs still need a while to evolve hands, while octopuses need to function a lot better on dry land."

"Well, it's not like they have recorded history to begin with or even language to tell their descendants to wreak vengeance on great apes," Diana said. "Once upon a time, our ancestors were ready snacks for leopards and lions, but cultures just look for convenience when it comes to livestock."

"Do you think Atlantis exists underwater?" I asked. "Or if the gods would make contracts with other species if they evolved enough intelligence?"

"Just focus on your fight with Simon," Diana answered.

I nodded as I popped an octopus fragment into my mouth. It was marginally better than the grubs a couple of weeks ago but required much more chewing. Even though Diana had been generous enough to encourage me to continue my journey, in the end, I still was awkward enough to put a strain on any friendship.

I brushed up after dinner with some basic boxing training, still unsure of any particular strategies I could use against Simon. I'd honestly lucked out on most of my fights so far, and I didn't think that I could do the same in the upcoming battle. When I woke up, I felt an odd writhing in my stomach, as if the tentacle bits were beginning to reform instead of being digested. I clenched both my hands, balling them into fists and spreading the fingers again, but I couldn't even manage to turn a single finger into a tentacle. When I held up my right arm and flexed my forearm muscle, however, I was able to create a jagged lining of diamond. Having hardened limbs and quick toes would be enough to force Simon to keep his guard up, but I doubted it would swing the tide in my favor.

I shared the small coliseum room with Diana, Inder, and Latis, and they all noticed as I tried to wriggle while looking at myself in the mirror. I'd managed to capture some part of the octopus so automatically last night, but now there was nothing going for me. Latis chuckled in amusement and clapped me on the shoulder.

"As clumsy as you are, I'd still rather have you around than Simon, Abyss," the spiky-haired boy said encouragingly. "Simon would be competent and reliable, but also a bit too boring for an adventure's quest."

"Well, since you got the free meal last night, we can use some of our budget on breakfast," Inder said. I still hadn't been told how the money system worked anyway. I wished things could just be like a video game where an enemy would drop resources after its defeat or when some cash could always be found through side quests.

"This isn't going to be it," I insisted to my three companions as we shared a typical American breakfast. "To keep Latis amused and to help Inder and Diana's fates . . . somehow, I'll try enough times that I'll figure it out."

"Even if it comes to the worst, I'm sure you'll do fine, both as a hero and in the mortal world," Inder said. Diana elected to stay silent. She apparently didn't want to risk another weird conversation about our food and livestock enacting revenge on humanity.

The stadium I was herded into was around half the size of a basketball court, which was a large enough space for two combatants to move around and shift position. I wanted them to add a few decorative pillars that I could figure into a strategy. It would be even better if I could jump between buildings or through tree branches. An open field meant that Simon could teleport wherever he pleased without risking a fall.

"In the red corner, we have the leader of the Western Sanctuary, the one who has completed over a dozen Quest Transfers, the teleporting hero, Simon Williams!"

Clerics and heroes alike had laid down their arms to witness this event and cheered to celebrate the favorite. Simon was wearing a chainmail shirt and shorts, but aside from that, he appeared to prefer mobility to defense.

I wore my usual tunic and shorts, and my newest sandals were still broken at the toes from the times I used the Diamorph transformation on my feet. "And in the blue corner, we have the upstart young boy who contracted with the legendary Witch herself, the diamond-sprouting, beast-mimicking marvel, Abyss!" I was surprised to hear that the cheers for me were only slightly softer.

"Your mind hasn't changed, has it?" Simon asked as he scanned me from head to toe. "Dorothy decided to tag you. She's done that to only two other heroes that I've taken quests from. Those were much harder battles than the rest, and with your power and your spunk, you might be the hardest."

"Trying to lower my guard with flattery?" I asked.

"More like trying to empty your bag of tricks," Simon said.

"With introductions out of the way now," the announcer continued. "Let us see whether Abyss' quest is worthy of transfer!" The crowd cheered once more, and Simon wasted no time. He was aiming for an instant knockout.

I burst four fresh Diamorph claws in my right toe and leapt out of harm's way just as Simon's fist grazed my ear. I was leaning forward slightly, and a heavy counterweight was extruding from my lower back that I hadn't noticed before.

"He's as nimble as a cat, our beast-boy Abyss!" the

announcer declared, and much of the crowd burst into laughter.

"Even the greatest of boxers wouldn't be able to fight a lion," Simon said as he circled around and bounced on his toes. "Even if you're missing a couple hundred pounds of muscle and force, I'll have to teleport a lot to deal with you."

Keeping my balance and form with my bottom half made it hard for me to create diamond knuckles or turn my fingers into claws, but I still had to press my advantage while my focus lasted. I burst forward, nimbly changed position and angles, and searched for weak points in Simon's guard. Even without teleportation, the tall redhead knew how to guard, bob, and weave, and while I had impressive speed, I still threw fists like an amateur lightweight.

I knew it probably only lasted less than a minute, but trying to carve through Simon's guard felt like a full ten hours of intensive labor. Finally, I managed to score a hit on his thick beard—unfortunately, that was when he decided to counter by teleporting toward my blind spot.

Out of the corner of my eye, I could barely see Simon's punch directed at my left temple. He again aimed for a quick knockout blow. I stumbled backward quickly and hardly got my guard up in time to block his next strike. When the dust settled, we were a good three or so meters away from each other, and while I was sweating from the intense effort, Simon remained calm and composed, undeterred from the hit I'd scored on his cheek.

The crowd erupted enthusiastically. "The beast-boy scored a hit!" the announcer declared. "Something we haven't seen in a long while against Simon! But it appears he needs some reminder on punching technique . . ."

Simon shook his head. "You've progressed for sure, Abyss, but at this point, you merely augment strength and speed and disregard stamina. In addition, there's a battle going on in you, the human fighting against the other species in your possession." As if on cue, the remnants of the octopus I'd eaten last night jumped up in my stomach as if it was preparing to piece itself together.

Simon was planning to merely wear me down in a battle of attrition. If I didn't use my Diamorph transformation, he could easily knock me out by teleporting to my blind spots. But now I could see why cats were so lazy, as my ankles, toes, and the mutated claws felt as sore as if I had been jogging for over an hour.

Then I just had to catch Simon off-guard, right? I tried to shift the squirming tentacles in my stomach toward one of my arms, but all I could feel was itchiness in my lungs and spinal column. I had managed to create a giant spring and a protective net before—but the former was too slow and obvious, and the latter seemed dependent on having been on an oil field. I had no idea how octopus biology worked, but I could only hope that the tentacles crawling through my organs would eventually come of use if I just kept fighting.

"Are you really okay with your current path?" Simon asked. "Many heroes and Witches fail when their powers are pushed to the brink. You might have the protection from death itself, as life finds limitless ways to adapt and evolve, but would you be fine becoming a monstrosity, an aberration of species, instincts, and brains, and all?"

I chuckled at the thought and faked confidence. "Hero stories are my favorites, so I don't plan on turning into an eldritch horror anytime soon." I pounced forward off of my hind legs, and as I did so, the rumbling in my organs died down a bit. The same process began to repeat itself, and although the crowd definitely enjoyed it, I was quickly getting exhausted. Even if Simon would never have the speed and reaction time to deal with my nimble cat-legs, he would bob and weave just enough so that when I finally got around his guard, I could only graze his chin and cheeks, just like the first time. And whenever I got that deep, he would quickly counter, which left my poor legs with more soreness with each passing minute.

I had to fake it and act a little wild, just as Dorothy would. I swung around with a wild haymaker when Simon teleported. It would be an easy dodge for someone of his experience, but I didn't plan on ending it there. "Don't be Deku!" I yelled as I shifted the carbon and muscle in my legs. Even if I hadn't ever seen them at the zoo, there was at least one famous animal I knew that could deliver a mighty kick . . .

Thud!

Even though Simon had his guard up, I heard the sound of bone snapping as both of my heels found their target. As I landed on my side and rolled over, I could see Simon stumbling back from raw shock. Luckily, while I was regaining my strength and balance, Simon was also busy trying to pop his arms back into place, using his magic for healing rather than offense.

"And we've got a kangaroo kick!" The announcer yelled, and the entire crowd cheered. "Just like in Australia! But Simon's far from done, even if his arms are damaged!"

I found that my legs were now extremely wobbly as they tried to go from the hop-and-kick patterns of a kangaroo to the flexibility of a cat, or at least my old human self.

Simon had recovered and healed first, and he was walking toward me slowly. "You're just making this harder for yourself, Abyss," Simon said. "I'll have to fight you until you pass out and stop moving."

"It's my quest . . ." was all I could mutter. I felt short of breath as I stumbled forward and realized that I probably couldn't even throw another good kick. Simon would just grab my leg and snap it with his strength. I noticed that the tentacles had finally found their way to my upper body and that suckers were sprouting on my palms and inner forearm.

All I had to do was land a grab and then hopefully suffocate or squeeze the air out of my foe with my other limbs.

Simon could see that strategy from a mile away. Now that my legs were out from under me, he was free to teleport as often as he wished. The first fist that rammed into my cheek sent me spinning and flying. The crowd was going crazy now that the fight was nearing its climax, and the noise echoed across my throbbing ears and head. Luckily, I could still pick myself up and stumble upright—I had either developed more stamina or the soft, flexible skin of an octopus, or Simon's arms just lacked his normal strength due to injury.

"This is bad for our underdog, folks!" the announcer said. "It appears he can no longer modify his legs! But let's see if beast-boy has one last trick up his sleeve!"

"So what if I'm a monstrosity?" I asked Simon. I wasn't sure if the last hit had scrambled my thoughts. "Nothing's more boring in stories than an unbeatable guy with a sword or a guy that could solve everything with friendship and fisticuffs. Hero stories should have endless potential, even if that means endless weirdness . . ."

"Everything still has its place, both in stories and in the environment." Simon surprisingly gave me a serious response. "Introducing new species to ecosystems often causes mass extinctions, and many rapid mutations result in needless suffering. Do you think you can just roll around in radiation and become *Spiderman*?"

My brain was getting fuzzier and fuzzier by the second, as if more of its attention was being diverted into my two modified arms.

"At least have the sense to jest . . ." I muttered. I was half-slurring. "I've got the current . . . Octo-ward . . ."

This was bad—from using the familiar cat-legs to the kangaroo kick to now a fresh pair of octopus arms, I couldn't control my own basic impulses. Simon teleported again and clobbered me in the gut once more, which sent me rolling across the dirt field. I could feel my ears twitch as time seemed to slow. Drool pooled out from my jaw, and I estimated the next blow I took might make me retch.

"You just can't bet against Simon, right?" one of the audience members asked.

"Can't blame an old geezer for wishing for something new, right?"

"It's not over!" the announcer argued. "Never count out this young upstart!"

As my vision began to clear up, I saw that the suckers on my left arm were all gone now, and this was as far as the tentacle transformation would get me. Perhaps if Diana had taken me fishing through my first few days instead of going through the grasslands and forests . . .

"Abyss, get up," I heard a voice whisper. "Aren't you going to keep your promise to me?"

And Simon? Simon wouldn't care too much about Diana or Inder. They weren't priorities in the larger world of heroes and villains, right?

"And he's back up to his feet, folks!"

Even though my legs were numb, I stumbled upward and raised my arms to face Simon.

"Although it looks like he doesn't have suckers on his arms anymore, Abyss is truly willing to give it all to entertain us!"

"Don't despair, Abyss," Simon said. "You have plenty to live for when you return to the mortal world."

The mortal world, I thought to myself. What was the best I could do—become a biologist or chemist trying to develop a questionable new drug or pesticide? But scientists merely studied impartially and haven't yet reached raw experience. I would always cling to a semblance of my human brain, for better or for worse. But even if the suckers on my arms were gone, I still felt that the second subset of my brain was moving around and swimming between my organs.

The octopus parts I'd eaten last night were resurrected and ready to burst out any second. It didn't want to share control with my human brain and fight over my arms and legs. But it also wouldn't pop back into a full living being after leaving my body. It was just a foreign thought, a wild curiosity of being—something that had so perfectly evolved as both predator and prey . . .

"You're not listening, are you?" Simon continued. "Looks like I should end it before you completely lose your mind."

When Simon's next fist hit me in the center of my chest, I transferred all conscious power into the second brain that had formed. Dark blue tentacles erupted from my chest and wrapped their suckers around Simon's right arm. They were as slimy as an octopus that had just been submerged in water, and I could control at least six of the tendrils. Simon's attempts to pry the tentacles away with his free hand were to no avail.

"What a shocking development!" the announced exclaimed. "This might just be what the beast-boy needs to pull the upset!"

"You've only strengthened my resolve," Simon insisted as the tentacles from my chest grew larger and longer. "I'll wait for these tentacles to dry up if it means wrestling this dangerous power from immature hands."

Now, with the extended tentacles, I had some mobility and was up a limb when it came to fighting against Simon. Even if my arms were much shorter, two functional arms were greater than one, and if I could just harden and strengthen the muscle enough, I could pull the upset.

Desperate to escape my clutches, Simon teleported and sent me into a dizzy void as I rocketed across the gaps in space-time. "Orrhrhauuuoooh . . ." I groaned. I felt all my organs shake and jitter in the short trip. My tentacles had allowed me to travel alongside Simon during the short spell and negated his attempt to shake me off.

"Imagine that the one thing I needed was salt," Simon said. I was really lucky that he wasn't able to teleport individual body parts like Dorothy could.

Now many in the crowd began to jeer. "He's taking away Simon's power! This isn't a fair fight!"

"Silence, peasants!" A familiar voice boomed. It took me a while to put my finger on it, but I realized that it was Melosh, the cleric who had attacked the Western Sanctuary. "Simon, the Witch Dorothy, and the high clerics all agreed upon the conditions of the Quest Transfer. If your red-haired hero can't even shake off an abomination from the sea, then too much faith was placed in him to begin with."

"Give it up, Abyss," Simon said as he sent me through another short teleportation trip. I tried to land punches on him while his ability was on cooldown, but I knew it would take a very long time to knock him out. "You can't possibly lead the heroes and Witches against the clerics without my assistance. You won't even manage to save your friends, who you care so much about."

"This is only the beginning," I insisted. "I may look like an idiot with tentacles sprouting from my chest now, but the future holds no brrsmeaaa . . ." I noticed my words were quickly slurring as my attention shifted from my brain to the tentacles. If I tried too hard to argue, I would lose my grip on Simon's arm.

The next time I was sent hurtling through space-time, I again saw a faint glimpse of the aether. Right now, I was too stubborn to stop fighting, but bits and pieces of the future fell into my vision. I tried to shake it off as a nightmare, a false fate, but things could never be that convenient. I could see Latis trapped as he crawled through a fiery inferno. Inder was a ghastly shell of herself as she cleaned and polished an endless row of icy mirrors, which each held a different death in the past and future. And Diana wore a metal collar and spiked weights on her ankles – she was dragging herself along as the resurrected Pharaoh stood over her. And if that wasn't enough, I began to see Simon's past, filled with accomplishment and victory.

If my story was that of a struggling, undisciplined writer's, Simon's was a classic high fantasy that could stand alongside *The Lord of the Rings*. He won over many allies, saved many innocents from disaster, and defeated devious villains, minimizing harm like a true hero would. Was it a single story at all, or was it a culmination of the high points? Horror and tragedies had always been acceptable forms of entertainment, but I was warped and sinking quickly. If Simon was a diamond that carved and polished itself, I was an endlessly churning pool of fossil fuel that was just waiting for humans to exploit.

But that was why I had to win this battle, I thought as my mind synced back together with the octopus' tentacles. My vision started to clear up as I threw clumsy punches left and right at Simon. Humans had a rather foolish tendency to preserve and isolate beauty and make the beautiful a mere lie and escape. To have a larger world, a larger universe resulted in being eternally lost, to admit the endless roads that were yet to come and the memories that were gradually fading. Simon might be able to better control my power if he took my quest, but he could never delve as deep into the swarm of beings that gnawed and thrashed through the chains of life.

"So you revel in selfishness after all," Simon said. "You saw your future failure and chose to embrace it as long as it meant experiencing more change, more power." Simon was finding it more and more difficult to block my strikes with his left arm, and my wild swings began to gain more legitimate form. "The loser of this transfer ceremony will be banished to the mortal realm for eternity, they say. But I've taken quite a share of Dorothy's magic through my contract, so I expect to see you again someday, Abyss. Maybe I'll witness your full transformation into a monster."

"And Simon's faltering more and more!" the announcer declared. "Is this the grand upset we've all been waiting for?"

I drowned the words out of my mind as the crowd continued to clamor. I might regret this decision forever, as it might be the only chance for me to return to a peaceful life. I don't know whether it was my decision, the octopus' brain, or any of the creatures that had found their way into my digestive system one way or another. One last solid right punch rendered my redheaded foe unconscious as he fell back. It took me a few minutes to get off of Simon, as the octopus tentacles didn't volunteer to detach themselves. They might have still thought the fight was going on as long as he was still breathing.

"And it looks like Simon really is out for good!" the announcer said. The crowd was as chaotic as ever as I struggled to detach the tentacles from my chest. Every time I tried to pull the squirming mass away, it felt like my heart was being squeezed dry. I had hardly any strength remaining after the battle, anyway, so I got up to my feet and turned to the crowd with the writhing tentacles on full display. "Here is the champion standing, the beast-boy who shamelessly shows his tentacles, Abyss!" the announcer continued. "The Western Sanctuary for heroes and Witches will need a new leader now, and Abyss will finish the quest that was given to him and seal the God of Fire!"

I wondered how long it would take for me to master Simon's power and teleport on a whim. I looked around the crowd to see a wide variety of expressions. Aside from cashing in on their bets, I could see everything from worry to amusement at the fact that this inexperienced kid had just taken out the protection for the Western Sanctuary. In fact, I wondered why Melosh and the clerics weren't just stomping in and killing all of us heroes.

"Don't be too impatient, everyone." I could see Melosh and some of his golden-armored allies discussing among themselves. "We agreed to a ceasefire until the beast-boy fulfills his quest and seals the God of Fire. Once he completes his quest, we'll then vanquish the Witches and their monstrosities."

So at least I wouldn't have to worry about them. But there was still Captain Drake and his ragtag men who had managed to steal a kidney and some of my ribs. I didn't worry about it that much back then, but if I had managed to sprout a separate octopus-brain, it would be a very real chance that I'd have to face an augmented clone of myself. Even just imagining the situation was making me dizzy. My feet were still sore, and I realized that I was going to land on the hard dirt as I fell into half-consciousness.

"They're off of his chest now, but you have to be patient for me to remove the rest of the mutation." I could hear Dorothy's voice as my eyelids began to stir.

"Was this your doing?" Diana demanded the Witch. "You had dozens of opportunities through your long life to rework your contract, but why the fascination with Abyss? Are you doing this to one-up the legendary Witch?"

"Can't a girl keep her secrets? I've given many heroes and adventurers alike ways to proceed on their quests. Abyss-boy here just made the most of it. But rather, you should be surprised at yourself. I don't think you've shown this much concern for a hero in two centuries, Diana."

I finally mustered the strength to open my eyelids and found a pair of wet lips planted to my forehead. It would be flattering if it was just a friendly kiss, but . . .

Slurrrp!

Dorothy pulled back from my head and chewed on the strand she'd just sucked out of my skull vigorously. "Space-time magic can only be nullified this way," she said. "I merely made the octopus that you ate forget it was food, that's all." I felt my forehead and noticed that a scab was quickly forming. I also had massive scars brushing against my clothes—apparently, I'd been changed into a fresh new outfit since falling unconscious.

"Since I beat Simon, does that mean that I have his quest now, or at least get some of his powers?" I tried to teleport left and right, but I remained in the same resting place and likely looked like an idiot while I expected something to happen.

"Heroes can only manifest a certain amount of power," Dorothy said. "If you would be able to teleport with Simon's finesse, that would probably mean that you'd have to give up your current powers." The Witch reached out and felt my forehead again, checking to see if she'd really removed the octopus remnants. "And if you just gave up your current powers for something more convenient . . . well, the Witch you contracted with wouldn't be too happy with that."

"But you'd decided that it was time to give up on Simon," I said. "Shouldn't she have at least made me skim through a few terms and conditions before deciding to give me such an important quest?"

Dorothy shrugged. "I'd love to have more tea parties with you and try to knock out these boring sensibilities, Abyss, but you should keep going with your quest. The longer you wait, the more difficult it will become to hold the God of Fire within the dungeon."

"Can you give me something to at least make my future quests easier?" I asked Dorothy. "You know, a bag of winds or a magical fortune cookie?"

"If you really need it, I'll give you a talking head," the Witch replied.

Again, with another bizarre suggestion. I wondered if Dorothy would become even crazier the next time we met without Simon to counterbalance her as the chosen hero.

"Oh, don't look at me like that," Dorothy said. "I'll be excited to see you grow, both on the inside and the outside. When that happens, Diana, you'll no longer have to worry about him. Unless you'd want him all for yourself, huh?"

Inder and Latis had now entered the small infirmary. "Abyss, I'm glad you're okay . . ." Inder began. Latis seemed more amused and impressed than he had ever been since meeting me.

"Did you two make the binding chains?" Diana asked. She was apparently shrugging off Dorothy's jests.

"We only got two, so we can split ourselves three to one or two and two if things come to the worst," Latis said. "The worst-case would definitely be leaving Abyss or Inder alone. Even if our beast-boy managed to come out on top here, he's always exhausted after every battle."

"Let's get to the ship," Diana suggested. "We'll continue this discussion there, as we still have at least a few hours to reach the island where the dungeon manifested."

As our small party of four reached the docks, I felt an edgy glare on my back. Justin, the wordsmith hero, had been waiting for my departure and was trying his best to hold back his outrage. "You'll never replace Simon, not even as a hero, much less as the leader of our Western Sanctuary," he said. "Once you're done with your quest, you'll be lucky if you ever serve as a useful puppet for me."

I tried to shrug off the sentiment, but I couldn't help but feel like he had a point. Simon was tall and handsome, and when I peered into his memories, he had always been composed and mature. But I didn't want to fall into Justin's traps, and I didn't want to start internal conflict among the heroes and Witches anyway. I could only hope that I had a warm welcome back at the Sanctuary once this quest was finished.

"So the binding chains, will they ensure that we stay together?" I asked as the four of us got back into the long Viking ship.

"As long as the members being bound remain alive," Inder explained. "We didn't prepare it when we met up in the mutagenic fog, and the pirates just sort of came out of nowhere."

"The labyrinth will destroy an isolated person very quickly," Latis said. "And it's almost guaranteed that we'll be split up after descending the first few floors."

"If the God of Fire is so powerful, why does he let a couple of chains prevent his emergence and victory?" I asked.

"Because he's on the insane side, remember?" Diana asked. "He's insane enough to always leave room for failure, just like the God of Ice has to play by his own rules and only dominate half of the universe."

It still didn't quite make sense to me, but if I could avoid being isolated, that would be for the best.

"Inder can help Abyss recover if he exhausts himself in a fight, since she carries the most medicines," Latis continued. "But we saw how badly that pairing went within the mutagenic forest. I wouldn't mind having to deal with Abyss, and if you're willing to risk an unknown spawning point and a random sacrifice, Diana, we can do a three-and-one split."

"Let's do two and two," I insisted. "I want all of us to come out of this alive." I didn't tell Latis about the vision I'd seen during my fight against Simon, but I had no idea how to prevent that nightmare anyway.

"I'll go with Abyss," Diana said, to my surprise. It was difficult to tell if she was blushing through the black markings on her cheeks. "Given my shooting skills, I can pick off a lot of threats from a distance, and once we get in really deep . . . well, I might be just what this idiot needs to go into overdrive, just like it was with our fight against Bethany and when he fought against Grigory." I'd also seemed to hear Diana's whisper when fighting Simon, but it really might've just been a hallucination.

"Latis and I can handle ourselves," Inder said.

The spiky-haired boy nodded with a slight smile. "I'd rather deal with my half-sister than someone whose last line of defense is sprouting tentacles and suckers."

"Well, animals didn't evolve to entertain humans," I shot back, but I was surprisingly taking the joke well.

And so, the binding chains were set up, tied to our wrists, and conveniently lightweight. They appeared to be semi-transparent links of pure energy. "We'll have enough flexibility to fight in these, but their strength is also their weakness," Inder said. "If you try to distance more than six or seven meters from the partner you're tied to, they'll pull you back and hinder your movement . . ."

"Incoming!" Latis yelled as he swiveled the steering wheel and fumbled the oars about. The waves had been getting more and more violent, and now they were enormous enough to capsize our boat. The four of us all rowed to the left and found calmer waters, but we had no viable path to approach the dungeon we had to conquer.

Latis appeared to be cursing under his breath, but once Inder joined suit, I realized that he was performing an incantation.

"If you can use even a fraction of Simon's power, now's the time to try it," Diana said. "Those two are calling for their father, the God of Ice himself, to calm the waves enough so that we can reach the dungeon."

"Like . . . how?" I asked, bewildered. Another violent wave smashed against our ship, and as I turned and flinched, I saw a squeaking, smiling cetacean tumble through the air.

"Aeeearaaeeaeaea!" the dolphin squeaked.

"Uh . . ." I started. I scratched my head and tried my best to comprehend the animal. Dolphins were intelligent enough to at least have some form of rudimentary language, but I couldn't understand a single word.

"Abyss!" Latis yelled. "Stop sightseeing and help us stabilize the boat!"

The dolphin's squeaks began to echo in my mind as the world around me turned into murky shadows. I still couldn't understand any of the creature's language, but the familiar pain in my abdomen flared up again. And here I thought that Dorothy had fully removed the octopus . . .

"So I meet the one that would curse the world for the sake of heroism," a voice whispered in my head. I was now in an endless hall of mirrors, with each one of the many reflections made of perfectly polished and sculpted ice. The voice seemed oddly familiar somehow, as if I was talking to myself—was this my future self, who stood in the shadows between the endless mirrors? The figure was surprisingly tall, almost as tall as Simon might be, and looked at me with broad, muscular shoulders. I suppose a future growth spurt wasn't too out of reach, even if I had been short my entire life.

"Um, hi," I said. "I don't know where I was just dragged into, but will you help us reach the dungeon so we can seal the God of Fire?"

"Requests, always starting with the requests," the man said. "And here I insisted on avoiding humanity. Such feeble-minded beings, and yet they were yet another species chosen by the God of Fire to bless magic upon."

"Could you be the God of Ice?" I asked as I tried to remember the metaphysics of the universe that had been detailed to me. "Shouldn't you be more powerful than the God of Fire? Can't you just . . ."

"I should be more powerful than him, and in the long run, I will still be victorious," my future self said to me as he began to walk forward. The shadowy mists fell off of his body, and I saw that the man wore jeans and a black T-shirt. His face and skin were marred with black linings, of which some were pulsing a heated red from the energy. "If I had gotten my way from the beginning, life itself would have never begun from the pool of amino acids and proteins, not on Earth or any of the other planets in the universe. In the beginning, all were one, and there was only me in such being. But the nature of chaos itself started to split things apart. The one force became gravity, electromagnetism, and the two nuclear forces, while endless elements began to mix around after the first elements. It was all well and good in my eyes, for even in a more complex universe, the laws of physics still held supreme."

"Does the explanation really have to be this long?" I asked.

"You seemed curious enough to learn about the origins of the universe, so I'm giving you a brief account," my future self said bluntly. Of course, it wasn't the explanation I'd wanted—it wasn't the explanation that any human would want. "Alas, the constant ebb and flow of new stars and galaxies wasn't enough for the God of Chaos and Fire. It was no more than a nonsense force that never should have existed, and yet it created life itself. The existence of a being that predicated on its own death and end."

As the words left my future self's mouth, the sharp pain in my abdomen and organs bolted up again. This time, I wasn't feeling the octopus specifically, but all sorts of noises—chickens and pigs, cattle and fish, all of their protein, fat, and energy that I'd absorbed were demanding to be reborn. "And that wasn't enough for the God of Fire? He wanted to select a few species that would dance more with magic?"

"All species have to develop a certain level of intelligence before even being considered," my future self explained. "More intelligence meant more strategies and possibilities and more ways to self-destruct, to contradict, and to collapse in sorrow. For many planets, it's enough for life to emerge and never evolve the necessary sapience. I held back the God of

Fire with all my might before he finally managed to deal with humans. And it appears he's content with his choice to this day, going so far as to allow a human like you to remove his seal and become his personal puppet."

I scratched my head once again. "So both the God of Fire and the God of Ice lack any concern for our welfare? Certainly, there's a third party like you might've created a descendant with the interest of all sentient beings in mind . . ."

"Intelligence and complex emotions, as you might describe them, are only enough for us to take an interest in the same way a scientist might study organisms in a lab," my future self explained. "It flatters me, as the creator of the universe and its laws to know that humans are one of the few lifeforms capable of understanding said laws and history, no matter how rudimentary it's destined to be with their limited brainpower. However, the majority of human beings haven't changed. Even if they learn that scientific progress is the key to immortality, so many choose to be shallow hedonists."

"Well, if you built the universe in the first place, it's just another by-product of how neurochemistry has evolved, right?" I asked. "So that's not really our problem." I hadn't prepared for such a roundabout conversation.

"Whether it's to be a hero on a battlefield or a martyr, a saint for some deity . . . the God of Fire rules over *Homo sapiens* like any other life form," my future self continued. "Life can only exist and thrive in the face of self-destruction, even if that self-destruction is a grand illusion. Even if both of us, the God of Fire and I, the God of Ice, can understand both your brain chemistry and your emotional status, is there any reason for us to be concerned?"

I chuckled. "Well, you were concerned enough to talk to me and not kill me on the spot." As soon as those words left my mouth, the endless cycle of life and the food chain within my body once again began to stir about. This time, I wasn't feeling the pain of hundreds of farm animals begging to be uneaten and vying for my thoughts. It was more like I'd tripled the amount of nerve cells in my body, and they'd grown sensitive enough to detect even the slightest movements from my microbiome.

"Oh?" The God of Ice said as he ripped off his shirt and revealed a nightmarish diagram of exposed organs and muscle. "So that's how powerful your contract is with the Witch? Then I'll take an interest in you beyond this quest."

It was a sensation similar to the octopus arms, where another mind had sprouted from deep within me. Even if it wasn't direct pain, I could hardly move now that I could feel dozens of different species of bacteria chugging along in my intestines. "As . . . as soon as one dies, hero or villain, they're ready, aren't they?"

"A corpse, the product of death, is a breeding ground for many forms of life, in all shapes and sizes," the God of Ice returned.

"But I wonder if the bacteria currently living inside me would weep," I said. "They rely on me to provide them with, well . . . the dead cells of dozens of other creatures, don't they?"

"Indeed," the God of Ice said. "Perhaps I'm the fool for even bothering to intervene in your affair and dancing along to the overdramatic song of the God of Fire. Perhaps it's best to let the lot of you humans live like bacteria on a chaotic and unstable planet and let your worries dissolve alongside your intelligence . . ."

"I don't care if I'm playing hero," I announced. "And I don't care how much worse these . . . life struggles, power struggles within me will get. If I can save the lives that matter to me or influence those that I'll meet in the future . . ." I stumbled across a mental lapse as I found the foul taste of raw eggs and grubs in my throat. And even the delicious taste of a bacon cheeseburger was predicated on . . . I shook off the thought as quickly as possible. "I want to see the God of Fire and give him a piece of my mind."

The God of Ice seemed unimpressed. "It will come to worse things than a power struggle between undying animals, young Abyss. You might have to carry humanity's own wretched arrogance and escapism on your shoulders. For every beloved Odyssey, for every Fur Elise, mankind must imagine thousands of more disappointments that are best destroyed and ignored . . ."

The mirrors now lit up with different memories, hallucinations, dreams, and nightmares. Weakness and despair of every flavor lined the walls of ambition and creation until every hero failed to manifest, and people came to ruin. I remembered what Inder said about her being fated to dozens of different tragic deaths in these endless mirrors—was the chaos the God of Fire promised better than such gruesome fates?

"Bring it on," I said with a grim smile. I had experienced dozens of mediocre novels, games, and shows in the past, be it for school or in my spare time. "It's always better that humans create such oddities than live the simple lives of bacterium . . . or remain as stellar cosmic dust, as beautiful as stars might become."

"Very well. I shall still the waters and direct you toward the dungeon. But no further than that. I cannot give you any tips on defeating the God of Fire, so you must earn his respect on your own."

As the mirrors replaced their reflections with pure light and crystal once more, I heard the high-pitched squeaks of another flipping dolphin. "Did Abyss' mind really just . . ." Latis began.

"Looks like he's the chosen hero, all right," Diana said. The ship we were on was now in a steady patch of water, and the fog in front of us was beginning to clear up. The odd, woozy feeling in my muscles and organs had reset itself, fortunately, although I couldn't get the conversation I had with the God of Ice out of my head. In addition, every time I had a mental reminder of the constant connection between life and death, it became harder for me to stay in one mindset.

"How long was I unconscious for?" I asked as I stretched my limbs to see if anything was wrong with my body.

"You were just blanked out for around three seconds, although I could see that powerful magic was forming around your body," Inder said. "Defeating Simon must've given you the opportunity to speak with the gods . . ."

I relayed the conversation I had with the God of Ice as Latis continued steering the ship toward the island resting over the horizon. "I wonder why he didn't just have Simon defeat me if he wanted to guarantee restoring some semblance of order to this world . . ."

"Looks like Dad hasn't changed at all, but I'm surprised he bothered to take a human form for you," Latis said. I felt sort of bad for not confronting the God of Ice about Inder and Latis, but I'd been too lost in the origins of the universe and its philosophical implications. It was as if my brain had expanded beyond my concerns, beyond human concerns, as I'd desperately queried the God of Ice for answers. Or rather, the animals and bacteria that had helped formed me over time were all pulling my thoughts in one direction . . .

"The heroes almost always remain under the command of their Witches," Diana explained. "If Dorothy decided to favor you and you ended up being able to withstand her magic, both gods probably would have accepted the outcome." I shook my head. I had never really expected there to be a personal god to console and support me through life, but after meeting one of the two gods, I was thoroughly disappointed with the nature of the universe.

"Get back to powering the oars," Latis commanded as the ship continued to bob up and down the peaceful sea. "Hopefully, meeting Dad didn't turn you into a nonchalant ice sculpture." Latis was superficially making a bad joke, but it was obvious to me that he was hiding some personal disappointment.

Chapter Three

From the outside, the dungeon that the four of us had to conquer appeared more like a walled-off prison. It had many decaying and broken bricks and pillars, crusted with white and gray grime. I'd expected that we would at least strategize a little, but Latis dismissed that concern. "None of us have any idea what's in the dungeon, and we have to seal the God of Fire as soon as possible. Just move quickly and try not to fall for the more obvious traps."

"This is it? This is your best party? Okoffo, coffuee . . ." A tall, androgynous figure stood before us. With a bored, disenchanted expression, it was blocking the front entrance to the dungeon. It appeared to have strands of wispy, white hair that reached its ankles, but upon closer inspection, the hair was either a collection of large worms or small snakes. "Where is Simon? Don't tell me . . ."

"Simon's on a long-term vacation, so you've got beast-boy Abyss," Latis announced. I gulped and wondered if the Medusa-person would let us pass through without a fight.

"I destroyed my insides and outsides to seal the God of Fire here to get a third-rate hero who can't control his power?" the Medusa-person asked. "Ohuufuu, Olaaamo . . ."

I tried to vouch for myself. "I may be clumsy, but both the legendary Witch who contracted with me and Dorothy, Simon's patron, wanted me to . . ."

"Bad omen, what has the world come to?" the tall figure croaked. "Reee-myth, myth . . . herself, has she taken a liking to poorly written tragedy? Or have we all been under . . .

seal . . ." The Medusa-person began to sway and wobble before it fell over in exhaustion. The rows of tangled chains blocking the front door began to rust and crumble before they shattered into dust.

"We'll worry about her . . . him later," Diana said. "Right now, we've got a dungeon to conquer."

Even though it hadn't been formally decided, Latis and I took the vanguard while Diana and Inder would support us from behind. Just a couple of seconds after walking into a dungeon, Latis blocked a row of spears that had been ready to impale me from the left. I heard the rumbling just in time to duck underneath an enormous, bouncy ball that had just cracked the ground in front of me and sailed over my head.

"Here we have, we here have, have we here a proper dance?" A chorus of children's voices began to sing.

"With new heroes, no dear Simon, no one's crying . . ." The row of bricks underneath my feet began to lurch and crumble about.

"If we force them all to keep their balance . . ." I scrambled toward where Inder and Diana were, but the dungeon seemed to anticipate my movement, and a large gap appeared between the two of us.

"What is justice? Be delicious!" The voices turned into animalistic squawking as a flutter of angry chickens flew out from between the gaps in the walls. These animals were supposed to be the prey population, either for a hungry human or a wily fox, but dozens of chickens began to surround me without any regard for their safety. I knew that I couldn't simply exhaust myself this early in the dungeon, but with the countless beaks and claws ready to scratch out one of my eyeballs, I had no choice but to at least transform an arm.

"Get ahold of yourself, Abyss!" Diana ordered as I swiped about with my right arm. I sent feathers floating into the air as I swatted the birds this way and that. The floor underneath me was still unstable and wobbly, so I jumped from platform to platform while fighting against the swarm of chickens. My awkward maneuvering forced Diana to follow, and to my relief, she had a whole field of arrows ready and shot down two chickens that had been pecking and scratching at my cheeks. "I don't have unlimited arrows, you know!"

"What can we do against unlimited chickens?!" I asked.

"Find their source!" Diana suggested. Inder and Latis were occupied with another immediate task, and I didn't have the time to regain my composure and look carefully.

Then I had to use another Diamorph transformation to amplify my senses, if not my movement capabilities. The chickens were far too noisy for me to dare increase the sensitivity in my ears so that only left smell. I remembered how I'd borrowed the boar's snout within the mutagenic forest, and once I sprouted a similar snout, I collapsed onto my knees as I caught the scent of fresh bird dung.

So, even in a magical dungeon, there had to be the unpleasant existence of excrement. "Conserve your arrows!" I yelled to Diana. "I know how to locate them!" As I jumped across the shifting walls and pillars, I fought every urge to retch as the smell of the bird dung grew more and more powerful. In addition, the chickens seemed to be intelligent enough to notice that I was closing in on their nest and continued to tear away at my new set of clothes and scraped any part of my exposed skin. I wanted to look back out of concern for Diana, but I trusted the chains that Latis and Inder had bound us with.

"Hopefully, this'll do," I muttered as I saw that a pulsing, purple vein of muscle and slime was flowing into a sealed lab room. Many of the chickens that were following me had decided to fly toward the pulsing vein and were pecking and licking away at its folds to drink the residue. If my claws weren't long enough, I just had to make a big Diamorph fist and cut off the source of nutrients that was making these creatures enraged.

As I smashed through the pulsing vein, its grotesque, greenish-brown contents splattered everywhere like a high-pressure fire hose. Now, virtually all of the squawking chickens that had been attacking me fluttered over to eat the slimy contents of the vein, and I heard a loud metal *thump* from the insides of the nearby lab.

"Abyss!" Diana called as she descended from the platforms that had been above me. "You could've asked for a bit more cover, you know." I looked down at my clothes to see that I was covered in grime and feathers.

"Now's not the time for that. We have to worry about whatever's in the lab . . ." I started.

"Not cool, man," a skinny teen boy with a spiky, pineapple-like red ponytail said as he walked out the front door. In his hands was a large bucket of fried chicken, and it appeared he was chewing on a drumstick as he spoke. The boy crunched on the bones for a bit before looking at us. "Oh, Abyss came instead of Simon. So Dad wasn't just being crazy. That means I'll have a little more time to get in my afternoon snack, but it also means that my job will be a bit too boring . . . but I suppose I'll let you repair that vein and maybe even spice it up before I kill you."

I probably wasn't in my right mind after being attacked by dozens of chickens. In any case, I knew that I had to try some unconventional approach. "Shouldn't you be watching out for your health?"

"I made the most delicious fried chicken," the pineapple-headed boy said. "And thanks to that, I was the weakest and had to just follow . . . *uwah*! Why do I even bother talking? It's just a waste of what little sanity I'm allowed. Barnacles! Barnaby!" Just as I was about to interject, he shot an annoyed glance at Diana. "But you're even more annoying than the clumsy lucky hero in every popular story. Suppressing memory and emotion for how many years now?"

I stepped in front of Diana instinctively. "Barney-boy, don't take it out on her . . ."

"Get over that phase already," the boy I dubbed as Barney explained. "The only good knight is a fallen knight! Let her weep and moan like a healthy girl should!" Barney put two of his fingers in his mouth and whistled. A sharp, slightly audible sound flowed through the air, and an odd scent hit my nose. Diana fell to her knees, her face and skin flushed with a mysterious red.

"Diana!" I exclaimed. I couldn't talk reason into someone half-insane, so I charged at Barney recklessly.

"You aren't the one I need," Barney said as he reached into his bucket and pulled out a large breast-piece. With a simple flick of his wrist, the fried chicken hit me straight in the gut with enough force to topple me over. "Enjoy that as a parting gift. I've got to finish my meal first." Barney disappeared through the shifting platforms and pillars as I struggled to stand. The fried chicken that had landed on me felt as heavy as a bowling ball.

Diana's eyes were still glossy, having fallen into half-consciousness. "Snap out of it, Diana!" I yelled.

"Ah . . . *Gryash . . . PotecharoOmanstamatadublem, ist ran . . .*" This was bad. She was either falling into her native language or was half-spouting gibberish. I hoped that it was just the former rather than the latter.

"Uh, you're currently on a quest to seal the God of Fire. With me, Abyss, the Diamorph hero who contracted with . . ." My words didn't appear to be getting through as she shook her head.

"Should have just . . . let it . . . but again . . ." I closed my eyes and decided to try to push the limits of my transformative abilities. If I couldn't save Diana here, it didn't matter whether or not I could seal the God of Fire. I managed to amplify my sense of smell once more, except this time, instead of bird dung, the scent of freshly fried chicken hit me. As I found that my mouth was watering, I opened my eyes and slapped my forehead in frustration.

"Move along, kiddo," a gruff, hunchbacked man said as he walked out from behind the laboratory with a plate of chicken and waffles in his hand. "It's a shame you came here instead of Simon, but a job's a job. Can't believe I've been working for a god for forty years." The man had a mop and bucket by his side, and a hard hat dangled from his back alongside with many construction tools strapped to his chest.

"If this dungeon's magical, why do they need a janitor and repairman?" I asked.

"I asked the same question for over five years and didn't get an answer," the hunchbacked man said. "The God of Fire took a liking to human conventions, and one of those was having grunt workers around. Well, it's not like life would've been that much different if I'd been allowed to stay in the mortal realm. I wasn't a hero who got sent here as punishment, just a randomly picked mortal serving for the sake of amusement."

"Is there any way you can help Diana?" I asked. "I'm not sure what that Barney-boy did, but . . ."

"The archer girl who assists on heroes' quests?" the hunchbacked man said as he took a bite out of his chicken. "Let her stay like this for a while. I'd say Barney's doing you a favor as long as you can defeat him in the end." I restrained myself from walking up to the janitor and smacking him over the head. "I'm not sure why she's even with you this far in your quest. But she's a bad omen. If you stay with her for much longer, you'll be lucky to last another year."

"Are you really a janitor anyway?" I asked. "Or just a follow-up challenge to the swarming chickens, someone placed here in order to trick me?"

"I've learned to be content either way. And either way, I'm still a grunt for you to ignore," the janitor said without a hint of deception. "But I do worry what's going to happen if you don't manage to seal the God of Fire. Will I have to work non-stop and without sleep once the entire universe becomes mindlessly chaotic, or will I be able to resign and party like a mad idiot?"

"Okay, then can you tell me the quickest way to find the God of Fire?" I asked. "Since you've probably seen your fair share of dungeons during your employment . . ."

The janitor shrugged. "All I can say is to be careful once you descend the first flight of stairs. There's a rampaging goat-thingie causing a huge mess. That's why the chicken factory was moved all the way up here." The hunchbacked man winced as if he'd just heard a voice in his head. "Back to work soon." The man appeared pensive for a short while, as if he really did want to stay and chat for a bit longer. "There's plenty of fish in the sea, young lad, but . . . never neglect your heart. There's hardly a pretty girl or a new friend to be found at my age."

The man appeared to be a janitor for real and was now cleaning up the bones that had been too tasteless for Barney to munch on. He also was repairing the collapsed rubble that had fallen from the shifting platforms and traps. I took Diana in my arms and wondered exactly where to go from here. I had to cross my fingers and hope that I could find some sort of oasis or healing potion in this dungeon . . .

"Abyss!" I heard Latis yell from one of the platforms above me. "Did you really come all the way down here to chase some chickens?"

Latis and Inder descended from the platforms. Both appeared in much better shape than Diana and I were at the moment. "Well, they all attacked me, and um . . . this guy with a red pineapple hair, he was pigging out on some fried chicken . . ."

I expected Latis to be amused and toss out a cheap joke, but instead, his face was riddled with thinly-veiled malaise. "Was he skinny, and did he mention anything about his father?"

"He was half-rambling, but I expected everyone in this dungeon to have some screws loose," I continued. "I also met a janitor afterward."

"Janitor's not important," Latis decided. "It's pretty bad news if the Children of Fire have also awoken. He was the one who put Diana in this dazed state, right?"

"Yeah, I just wasn't able to defend her . . ." I muttered. "All I got was a piece of fried chicken thrown at me."

"The God of Fire is supposed to mingle with mortal affairs and create absurdities, heroes, and villains," Inder continued from where Latis was cut off. "He's never supposed to manifest as a human enough to . . . well, reproduce, like the God of Ice can. But having chaos be delayed is in itself a possibility for chaos. Thousands, maybe millions of the God of Fire's possible children were supposed to have died somewhere along the lines. We were warned about a few of them that might pop into existence should things get really bad . . ."

"Well, if we can bust our way through to the God of Fire, will that be enough to return Diana to normal?" I asked.

"We might have to switch up our entire strategy at this point," Latis admitted. "Inder seems helpless, but she'll be able to scrounge up enough materials with her magic to keep Diana's condition from worsening. And due to her sealed fate, she won't die until the proper time. If we switch the pairings . . ."

I shook my head. "I got Diana into this mess, and I'm getting her out. I know how clumsy I was with these chickens, and . . . overall, with the octopus tentacles, with the mushrooms, with everything. But I'll make it work."

Latis sighed. "The pineapple-headed boy, whatever his name is . . . well, he's more likely to come after me anyways. It might be best to stick with our initial pairings if that gets you to the God of Fire faster."

Inder was apparently making progress with helping Diana return to consciousness but still had a worried look on her face. "She'll be good enough physically, but after you ran into Barney and his spell, something's changed regarding her neurochemistry."

"I still don't get why he targeted her rather than me," I said. "I mean, I'm the one that can sprout tentacles from his chest and all, right?"

Latis shrugged. "Never underestimate what living for four millennia can do to one's resume," he said. Finally, Diana began to stir and roll on Inder's lap. I was relieved when she opened her eyes, and I tried to brace myself for the worst.

"Ah, I got hit so easily." Diana wore new emotions on her face now, as if she'd lost all of her cynicism and grit and was ready to start anew. "But now that I'm finally complete again, I can help you finish this quest . . . agh," Diana said as she held her forehead gingerly. "I'm sorry I can only come out like this, but . . . maybe it was for the better."

"She might have made a contract thousands of years ago," Inder said. "A lot of people, heroes or not, wish for a little more courage, humor, or patience when it comes to life. Altering neurology is usually a one-way thing when it comes to magic, but with the God of Fire involved, well . . ."

"You saw it when we first met, didn't you, Abyss?" Diana asked. "In our dreams where you met the Pharaoh face-to-face." It had been less than a couple of weeks ago, but now I recalled being able to eavesdrop on her memories.

"Yeah, and afterward, all I got was bumbling through space-time with Simon," I said.

"The reason why I failed so many heroes, well . . ." Diana

began sheepishly. I was so used to the cheetah-cheeked hunter being confident and direct that I was taken aback by how cute she was now. If she straightened her hair out and let it grow longer, she would easily contend with any typical princess. "It was because I ran away from my true power. It was too unpleasant to see hero after hero die in front of me, but to be completely honest, if Barney hadn't allowed me to emerge like this, there's no way you would be able to complete your quest."

What a twist, I thought to myself. I still knew I had to be wary of a trap, but before I could attempt to add to the conversation, rifts and cracks appeared in the ground, and the shifting platforms above us slid and shifted like a jigsaw puzzle. Diana clung to my arm before swiftly working with her ropes and made sure that we were tied closer than the magical chains provided. I turned to face Inder and Latis, but a column of boiling water sprouted from the cracks in the ground, which effectively formed a barrier between our party of four.

"We'll manage somehow!" Latis insisted. "Remember that you're the one that has to complete the quest!" I turned to the nearest platform beside me, only to have another wall of boiling water cut off my path. Diana had the better idea and dragged me to the left, and although we found a clear path, we both lacked a general sense of direction and were increasing our distance from Inder and Latis.

"Watch out!" I exclaimed as I blocked a bright yellow blob of acid with my shoulder. I sunk to my knees in pain as I felt the acid slowly dissolve my skin and outer muscles. I heard Diana nock an arrow, and in less than a second, her projectile whizzed through the air and found its target. A high-pitched, animalistic squeal filled the air as I turned and stumbled to my feet. As much as my shoulder and upper arm hurt, it would have been much worse if the blob of acid had made contact with Diana's head.

Sploosh!

I was a bit luckier the second time and jumped to the side as the acid blob hit where my left leg had been. Ahead of me were at least a dozen purple, octopus-like creatures bobbing in the currents of boiling water. Each of them was forming acid projectiles with their round mouths.

"I suppose we can't negotiate?" I asked. If these angry octopuses were being spiced up like the chicken swarm earlier, I hoped that I could once again find a simple solution. "I'll distract them." I turned to Diana. "I have more agility with the cat claws and can regenerate much easier if I take critical damage." I untied the rope that Diana had connected to my waist, and she looked at me with genuine concern. "You have enough arrows, right? If you don't, I'll . . ."

"I'll tell you when I'm out of arrows," Diana said. "I carry some extra arrowheads, and as long as we can scrounge for materials, I don't want you to recklessly use your transformations."

I'd never seen Diana in close quarters before and wished that I could just give her some of my Diamorph powers. I tried to shake off the mushy feelings in my heart and rushed into the fray again, much like any hero would. Luckily, my overall strategy worked, as the purple octopus-creatures mainly shot their acid at me, and it usually didn't take more than ten seconds for me to hear another whiz of Diana's arrows and a high-pitched squeak from the dying creatures. I noticed that my stomach was rumbling as I pranced through the platforms with my cat-legs. We hadn't brought much preserved food, and I doubted that the God of Fire would be generous enough to give us something to snack on.

"One's missing . . ." I started as I saw ripples of waves float from the boiling water. Whether it was instinct or luck, I lurched to the right just in time to dodge an acid spitball that would have burned a gaping hole in my abdomen. Unfortunately, the acid ball still burned the skin from my left side.

Before the octopus could sink back into the safety of the water, I rocketed forward and smashed its head to pieces with a strong right fist. And just when I thought that I'd saved Diana another arrow, I recoiled in pain. The octopus' guts had spilled all over my right forearm, and they were as hot and acidic as the spitballs that had been launched toward me.

"Abyss!" Diana called out as she jumped over the platforms behind me. I tried my best to force a smile through the pain in my arm and side, but Diana immediately unraveled her set of bandages.

"The injuries on my arm are a bit more serious," I said. "But at the same time, it'll probably be irrelevant after I augment it with my next transformation." Diana apparently had decided to go for my abdomen, as well, even if it meant up using more of her bandages.

"I'm down to four arrows," Diana said. "I tried to stock up ever since we left the Moving Restaurant, but they were pretty expensive in the coliseum. In the past . . . quests usually didn't last this long, and if they did, the heroes I assisted would usually stock up on arrows, as well."

"We'll find a way," I said as Diana finished wrapping the bandages. She might have rubbed powder or herbs on the bandages as they wrapped around my waist, as I felt significantly less discomfort there. Unfortunately, moving my right arm even a little caused the pain in my forearm to flare up. Right after beating Simon in an epic duel, I would have to be humiliated by these small enemies yet again. And if that wasn't bad enough, my stomach let out a deep growling sound.

"Rushing through the dungeon will get us killed," Diana said as she took out some of her preserved food. "If we look carefully, there should be something edible here." I munched on the salted meat and nuts tactlessly, and as expected, it only served as a cheap appetizer. My stomach continued to growl as we continued across the shifting platforms into a short hallway.

As the room ahead of us lit up with torches lining the walls and platforms, I sighed with relief at the fact that this place seemed far more stable. The platforms and bridges were usually less than two feet wide, so the two of us would have to balance carefully to avoid falling into the bottomless pit below. It would make combat particularly challenging, but as the first several minutes passed, we slowly descended down the unstable platforms, only accompanied by peace and silence. For a while, there was nothing more than the echoes of our footsteps coming back from the deep pit below. Then, a low voice started speaking.

"Oh creature of the savannas, of the mid-day sun and bright—

"What shall you do when overcome with the fear of night?" Around half of the torches in the room simply wisped into smoke and embers, and the room grew significantly darker. The voice was an inquisitive male voice with an odd accent.

"Light is fleeting, and darkness slays her,

"To which God will you make the prayer?

"Prayer is lacking for these somber embers."

Another half of the remaining torches went out, and shortly after, the remaining ten or so torches were extinguished one by one. It became darker and darker until, all of a sudden, there was nothing but shadows adorning the slight gray outlines of platforms. Even if we walked extremely carefully, we would constantly have to check the edges of the platforms with our hands in order to prevent ourselves from tumbling into the endless pit.

"I don't suppose we packed a lantern, as well?" I asked. I found that Diana was rummaging around with her rope again and re-tied the knot around my waist.

"There are a few creatures that can produce light," Diana said. "If you were able to just mimic the firefly . . ." It was a serious suggestion, but even this far into my journey, the only thing I could maintain was forming diamonds. "If it'll destroy your organs, you don't have to do so, but . . ."

"A few creatures that can produce light," I said. "But many that can thrive in the night and darkness. Whether it's night vision, infrared vision, or augmenting the sense of smell . . ."

Hsst . . .

It was very faint, but I jumped up at the sound, startling Diana as I bumped into her. "What's the matter?"

"I heard a snake," I said. "Normal snakes can be venomous and deadly enough, but I don't want to stick around to be prey for a magical one." I heard Diana instinctively raise her bow before she lowered it again, aware that it was useless in the fog of night.

"Well, if you can become part-snake, maybe you could manage to feel the platforms better?" Diana asked. "Um, Abyss? It was just a joke . . ."

Maybe it was just the darkness surrounding me, but I'd fallen into that endless realm of shifting oil and mindless hunger, of fangs constantly tearing at prey and flesh eating flesh. And my stomach gnawed once again after eating the snack that I'd been given. There were so many different species in the world, so many different forms of life, and so many different forms of food. *But why were so many chemicals poisonous? Why couldn't the stomach simply digest everything?*

I felt my heartbeat, and in the mysterious realm, felt the heartbeat of dozens of other species. Some of them were faster, like hummingbirds and scampering rodents, while others thumped at a snail's pace. Should I simply appreciate this body? For humans were able to be much more active than cats when they were forced to rest or snakes that had to constantly bathe in sunlight. But on the other hand, if I were a cold-blooded reptile, I wouldn't need to feed my incessant hunger. If I was a snake, I could perhaps even slither about in this forsaken darkness as I searched for light . . .

I had to remember that Diana was with me and that I was going to get her out of this accursed dungeon. The human eye was complex enough, and nature could never rapidly switch screens and outputs like a computer could.

But if I could only borrow another creature's eyes once again to finally move in this utter darkness . . .

Something rapid-fired within my brain. It was going to be as bad as sprouting the octopus tentacles from my chest, if not worse. I wondered if Diana, Inder, or Latis would stick around if I ever went blind.

"Abyss?" A bright shimmer of red and orange lit up in front of me, and I stumbled backward and almost fell off the edge of the platform. When I regained my footing, however, I could make out the shadows in front of me, as they all emanated a faint red glow against the black abyss. I turned back to the glowing blob that Diana had become, unable to discern any of her facial expressions.

"I hope my vision goes back to normal," I said aloud. I turned around to see that another snake was busy crawling along the walls, while a few mice and rats were scampering about. If this dungeon had enough to support even a few mice and rats, that meant that there had to be something edible down here, right? Unless they simply lived on the scraps of fried chicken that Barney tossed them.

"Heat . . . to see heat is a blessing," the disembodied male voice said as he observed my newfound ability. "Heat means movement, and movement means chaos and life. For once upon a time, when all forces were one, there was no heat. It was I who first brought nonsense and chaos to the world, young hero. I made the electrons dance in sheer probability, I made neutrons decay, and I even allowed the endless array of elements around us. To borrow a serpent's eyes is a mild feat compared to what you can accomplish, Abyss, and once you reach the end of the dungeon, be prepared to serve at my side."

"An audience with the God of Fire himself?" Diana asked. "That's even rarer than getting a weird poem." The God of Fire seemed to have no interest in Diana, however, and as I blinked twice, I realized that the infrared vision wasn't going away for now.

"I can make out the platforms up ahead," I told Diana. "I was able to borrow the infrared vision from the snake, and the platforms are slightly warmer than empty air. Something's flowing from beneath them, although they don't appear to be insects."

"I still can't see a thing," Diana said. "I'm holding onto you tight and moving slowly so we don't trip over each other and fall." She was still the same blob of bright light, and I saw no additional heat flush to her face. "Maybe you can sprout an additional eye for me to borrow?"

"I can hardly toggle my infrared vision at the current moment," I said. "I'm not even sure if things will revert to normal when there's light again." My stomach growled once again. "But we should get going before I pass out from hunger."

It wasn't quite what one had in mind when it came to a romantic date, but at least it gave me a rare opportunity to feel like a hero again. The traditional events tended to be a haunted house, a scary movie, or even a test of courage on summer breaks.

Here I was, staring at the subtle lights from the platforms, descending farther into the dungeon for what? To fight this half-insane God of Fire so I could live and go on for even more quests?

"Ow . . ." Diana bumped into my head and shoulders and sunk down to maintain her balance. "Don't just stop suddenly. Do you have to go to the bathroom or something? I can't see a thing so you can just pee over the edge . . ."

"I'm not sure we can afford to waste body fluids like that in this dungeon," I blurted thoughtlessly. "There's a narrow chasm up ahead, so I was just being careful." I wasn't lying about what was ahead of me, but I was still frustrated that I over-thought everything. "You say you've been assisting heroes with their quests for four thousand years," I said. "And in all that time, there wasn't one time were you had to maneuver in the dark like this?"

"Even on most nights, towns had a few lanterns in addition to the moonlight," Diana answered. "If we were in forest areas, we'd always try to keep a fire going."

I was worried that Diana might fall and trip as we walked across the narrow chasm, so I turned around and walked backward, warning her if she stumbled too far to the left or right. I was still surprised that the God of Fire hadn't rained down additional traps or enemies upon us. I probably couldn't fight well at all if I was only able to see in infrared, and Diana would be shooting wild shots in the dark. But this was probably just the calm before the storm.

The two of us probably spent a couple more hours slowly descending the dungeon in the darkness, and to my dismay, it seemed obvious that we would have to stop and rest. Luckily, near the bottom of this almost infinite descent, a torch lit up along the walls, and with it, I spotted a possible food source.

I ran over to the torch aimlessly as Diana followed, and my vision began to somewhat return to normal. Diana was still a bright blob of heat, but underneath the fiery torch, I could make out an odd, bushy plant with many jagged leaves and unstable twigs. It was buried in rich soil and seemed to be surprisingly healthy, given that it had been growing in a dungeon.

"Wait, don't just call any plant food," Diana said. "Remember what happened when you decided to ingest the mushrooms that Inder recommended?"

It definitely could be an elaborate trap just for the God of

Fire to laugh at my foolishness and desperation. But I was now incredibly tired and hungry from our long trek, and as usual, I always lost some of my frontal cortex whenever I triggered a Diamorph transformation. If we spent another full day in this dungeon without eating, I might have considered taking a bite out of Diana.

"It might be a gift from the Witch of the Forest, right? I don't think the God of Fire would settle for poisoning someone to death when there are so many other flashier demises for unlucky heroes."

With that said, I took a big handful of leaves with my left hand, trying my best to peel away the sticks and twigs with my right hand. Although the scars on my abdomen and shoulder had healed well, punching the octopus had been a pretty bad idea. As I munched on the leaves and pushed them toward the back of my throat, my sense of disgust immediately went to war against my hungry stomach. This was far worse than eating the writhing grubs and the raw eggs, as if the water and fiber had been squeezed out of the plant itself and replaced with more bitter toxins.

Diana sighed. "Plants don't want to be eaten . . ."

"I just modified my eyes after sprouting tentacles from my chest," I told Diana. "I'm pretty sure I can develop an herbivore's stomach to digest these if I try hard enough." I swallowed the first bitter mush of leaves and picked out a second clump. Diana sat down beside me and carefully observed what I was eating.

"Wait, I see . . . bones here as well, and they're all picked pretty clean. Here's the upper jaw full of buck teeth, like a rabbit was chewing on these."

"Then it's edible, no matter how gross it tastes," I muttered. Still, as the plant matter made its way down my esophagus and into my stomach, I felt woozy and uneasy, as if I was recovering from sudden seasickness. I wasn't hallucinating or seeing anything strange, but my stomach was simply having trouble adapting to the new food source. Perhaps my intestines and liver were being warned of the toxins that I would have to flush out. But I was still hungry and needed fuel to heal my wounds as well as replenish my energy.

Diana sighed. "You get to act like a hero for just a few hours, and then it's going to follow-up with others having to dig you out of the consequences of your reckless actions. It's a shame none of these plant branches will make good arrow shafts. I . . . what on earth is that?"

I was too lost in my disgusting meal to turn my head around, but I heard small scurrying footsteps from creatures no larger than rabbits. "I'm too woozy to fight," I said. "Can you get at least one with your knife, Diana, and prepare some additional food . . ."

Thomp.

Small feet rammed into my cheek, and powerful kicks from rabbit-like creatures began to rain upon me. Out of half of my vision, I could see rabbits with wrinkled, furious faces and muscular legs with bulging veins.

"Abyss!" Diana exclaimed as she swiped around with her knife. She was only able to make small cuts on the mammals as they continued to kick away at my face and chest, and almost forced me to barf out the plant matter I'd just consumed. I threw weak, lazy punches with my limited strength, and when a rabbit chomped on my right forearm, I spun around and collapsed in pain.

"Are you having a field day now, God of Fire?" I groaned. Poisonous plants and ambushing in the darkness would never be a preferable demise to getting beaten up by mutant rabbits, it seemed. Even if there were only five or so rabbits taking turns beating me up, they did what the flock of chickens and acid-spitting octopuses couldn't . . .

"Breeeeaoooah!" Thunderous hooves smashed against the pavement as I heard chambers and rooms around me unlock.

It was an all-too-familiar, half-neighing, half-bleating sound that I didn't think would come to help me again . . .

"Ibonus!" I yelled. My vision had cleared up just enough that I could make out the outlines of the horse-ibex hybrid. "I'm not sure if he can carry two of us, but get on his back!" As Ibonus pulled up to my position, he knocked away a couple of mutant rabbits with a powerful kick. "Hopefully, he can take us through the rest of the dungeon . . ."

"You rode this guy?" Diana asked in disbelief as she helped me to my feet. I was still hungry, so I peeled off more of the jagged leaves and stuffed them in my pocket and clothes. "Latis said something about it, but even if he's huge, I'm not sure if he'd be fine with me riding . . ." As if to confirm Diana's suspicions, Ibonus snorted as if slightly annoyed.

"She won't hurt you," I said as I walked up to the goat-like creature and rubbed his cheek. "She can't be any heavier than I am." I climbed onto Ibonus' backside and gestured for Diana to follow. Although my cheetah-cheeked mentor still expressed misgivings, she hopped on behind me and started working with her ropes, tying her waist to mine.

"Breeeaaeeeoeee!" Ibonus bleated as he galloped toward the secret chamber that he had just emerged from. He only seemed slightly slower than the first time I rode him, although I knew that both his mobility and stamina would be compromised by carrying an additional rider. The worst thing was that I was exhausted both by using infrared vision and from the indigestion caused by shoving the leaves down my throat. I tried to hold onto Ibonus' neck, but my lower body chafed and shook from the galloping.

"Just as expected from the God of Fire's maze," Diana observed. As we exited the tunnel, we escaped the dark and dank atmosphere and broke into an open field. Even with my poor vision, I could see that there seemed to be at least five different *suns* in the illusory sky above that showered the field with blinding light. The only things that managed to cast shade were plants swaying their enormous leaves in the wind. The flora here took advantage of the additional energy to grow to gargantuan sizes. As I remembered the first incident where Diana and I had to traverse a large field of giant carnivorous plants, I wondered if I had gained enough experience to duplicate that feat.

Cloppck, rnrkrkrnk . . .

Ibonus suddenly veered to the right as a sharp needle grazed against my left arm. When blood began to flow from my wound, I noticed that, as usual, I wasn't dealing with ordinary weapons. It was as if the projectiles were spines from a porcupine, and on top of that, they were trying to prepare my flesh for easy consumption . . .

"Can you steer me toward some more arrows?" Diana asked. "There are too many of these porcupine-bird things!"

I tried my best to modify my eyes again or even use the pig snout I'd managed to sprout previously, but I was still digesting and recovering. I could quickly tell that the flying porcupine creatures were aiming for me rather than Diana or Ibonus. This made it a bit easier to try my best to harden my skin and cover my head, but I couldn't form the smooth, sleek armor that I desired. Within the diamond crystals that I sprouted, there were a few strips of bare flesh on each arm, and as I sustained shot after shot from these flying foes, I found it became harder and harder to maintain my composure.

"Don't die on me, Abyss!" Diana yelled frantically. She suddenly squeezed herself against my back.

She really was flat compared to Inder . . . stupid me. Are these going to be my last thoughts, as well?

"Don't try to shield me with your body!" I replied as I felt another needle strike my left arm. The projectile wedged itself within the cracks in my Diamorph armor. "I'll find a way somehow . . . like always!"

"It's been a while since you've let out such a squeal," I heard the familiar disembodied voice call out. "He survived considerably longer than most of the other heroes who were cursed with your presence." With my partially infrared vision, I could now see the *heart* of this illusory field that we were galloping through and the magical veins that supported the sky, the suns, and these odd porcupines that swarmed around me. "Will you see it as another inevitable tragedy?"

"Diana, can you see it?" I asked her. "It's moving around a bit throughout the sky, between the networks of these five suns. If you can shoot an arrow and pierce it head-on, perhaps we'll advance to the next section of this dungeon!"

Diana shook her head. "I only have three arrows left, and the entire sky is too bright for me to see anything."

My injured muscles began to twist and turn, as if they were being eaten from the inside out by tiny worms. "He's made his way deeper into the heart, through courage and becoming ever-stranger," the disembodied God of Fire continued. "But will you sacrifice him to me, so keep the never-danger?"

"Oh, shut it!" I yelled at the God of Fire.

"But my insanity and nonsense were what you desired," he insisted. "An interesting life you sought to acquire, and Witches and heroes the world required . . ."

"I'll be fine," I insisted to Diana. "I've seen too many shows and played too many games with straight-up diabolical villains. If this God of Fire really is a fruitcake that I have to beat, I'll embrace the challenge . . ." My tongue's muscles began to tie up, and small quills began to form at its tip. Slowly, the poisonous quills that I'd been impaled with were going to work themselves up to my brain—and what then?

"It's not just the God of Fire you'll have to deal with," Diana said. She was still hugging me from behind. "If I help you complete your mission here, the Pharaoh is certainly going to be resurrected. He'll definitely make you a pawn, a slave, but given what you've shown so far, your fate will definitely be worse than death."

"Then . . . whether the world be magical or mortal, dictators and tyrants will arise," I said. "And maybe I won't be lucky or smart enough to be the hero that ends it. But if it takes two generations or twenty, I want to inspire more people before I die. I want to . . ." My voice broke down again as quills stabbed against my tongue. "See you as . . . well . . ." Using the last bits of sanity and thought I had left, I continued tracking the *heart* of the illusory field with my infrared vision, and I watched it as it danced between the veins and the suns. I didn't know how exactly I would get Diana to see what I saw, but it was my only chance, given that I couldn't reach the heart even if I grew wings.

"Abyss . . . I'm sorry," Diana said as I heard her nock an arrow. My adventure wouldn't end here then! The quills that were trying to carve through my skull temporarily faded away, and my vision began to overlap with Diana's. Our vision was blending as if the information from two cameras was being perfectly rendered in a computer. "Agh . . . it's right there, isn't it?"

Diana let loose her arrow as it soared through the air, but I noticed it was off by a centimeter as the *heart* moving within the sunny skies bobbed and weaved. I could hear that the God of Fire was shrieking with one of his many voices and minds. "Crap! Abyss, try to use my lock-on magic, as well. I only have two arrows left!"

"The Pharaoh was an odd one, as he broke my rules perchance. Every now and then, I give men a glance," the God of Fire continued to sing.

"And with the Witches' sorrow, he declared to be . . . the end of fools that idolize glee.

"But lacking what he needs to rise

"Is you, the hero, Abyss' eyes!"

"Lock-on magic . . ." I muttered. Diana's shots had been incredibly powerful and accurate, and I thought that those were just the upper-limits of training. I'd never particularly asked about her powers other than immortality, but it seemed that she could share the visions of her heroes. I didn't know what penalty her magic incurred either—perhaps I had been selfish and foolish after all—but just like the fight against Simon, a hero was supposed to say *so what* when confronted with the morally ambiguous.

"Thanks, Abyss . . . if you manage to defeat the God of Fire, take care of me." Diana let loose her second arrow, and this time, the mark found the heart dead-center. As the *veins* in the sunny skies pulsed, I could see that one by one, the five suns that were surrounding the dungeon began to fade and shrink away. The flying porcupines collapsed to the ground, and once they shed their quills, they began to scatter like enormous rats. We were back in a long, dark chamber full of torches and dusty walls, and Ibonus clopped his hooves impatiently.

"I think he wants us to get off." I turned toward Diana and found that she was slumped unconscious on my back. Quickly, I untied the rope that she'd bound to my waist and helped her off of Ibonus. So these were her immediate effects of using her magic and sharing her vision with mine. "At least the quills aren't trying to mince me to bits anymore . . ."

I looked around for hints and shortcuts, for the chamber that we were stuck in still seemed uncomfortably long. "Hey, God of Fire! Don't tell me that a single arrow was enough for you to quit with your sloppy poetry!"

I slung Diana's unconscious body onto my shoulder, stepped forward, and looked for hints in the walls.

Had Ibonus really tired that quickly underneath the blaze of the five suns? Why was he even here in the first place?

I turned back to the horse-goat hybrid and rubbed his cheek once more. "I know that you probably can't understand a single word of mine," I said. "But thanks again for getting us this far. I hope I can treat you to some good apples. Maybe find some, er, cute ibex babes for you . . ." The beast showed no signs of comprehending me, but I could guess his thoughts from his eyes. He probably wanted me to ride him solo the next time and not drag along a second rider.

"Wall, wall, where to look for hints . . ." I said as I ran my finger across the dust. Almost half a minute of searching the cracks and bricks led to nothing, and just when I was about to turn and leave, the wall spun open to reveal a secret chamber. We were now in a grand staging area, with cartoonish, masked dwarves surrounding a boxing arena. It was much smaller than when I was fighting in the coliseum, but this time, a different pair of fighters would be the show.

"Ah, you're late. Father wanted to test you with the Field of Five Suns in addition to the dark room, but I wanted to be the one to end you." It was Barney, the pineapple-headed boy, and within the confines of the boxing ring, he was fighting Latis. Even though Latis was equipped with his two knives and fast on his feet as usual, Barney fought back with nothing but his arms and legs. The skinny redhead made sudden jerking motions to throw Latis off. He mostly caught him off-guard with jabs, but he followed up this combo with a strong kick to Latis' stomach. "And it's a good thing you came here because that means I can finally end this spar of ours."

I turned to Diana and couldn't find an empty seat for her to lay down in. Inder came over to my side, and I noticed that she wore a set of weary eyes as she forced a smile. "So she actually used her ultimate technique with you . . ." Inder said as she took Diana from my arms. "Maybe we have a shot of clearing this dungeon after all."

"Will she be all right? I mean . . ." I began.

"She's just going through a headache from using that ability for the first time in millennia," Inder said. "Doing it means, well . . . she can no longer hide with the suppression pact that she signed long ago. Most of the nightmares she's facing have nothing to do with you. Although if you do defeat the God of Fire, I'll give you the warning again . . ."

"Something bad will fall upon me, right?" I said. Inder nodded grimly. "How long have Barney and Latis been going like that?"

"A few hours, but it might have lasted an eternity had you not found your way in here," Inder said. "But now that you are here, the chances of you completing this dungeon don't look bright either. Barney will unleash his full potential once you step into the ring, and you're bound to step in the ring eventually."

Before I could protest, the middle-aged, hunchbacked janitor that I'd seen earlier stepped in with a cart and a plate full of food. "Oh, Abyss-boy, you hunger, don't you? We've got some quilled bamboo rats to go with our signature homemade waffles! The masked dwarves decided to make this special batch for this occasion. Hope it serves as a final meal!"

"I don't plan on dying here," I said, but I took a full plate of fried rat and waffles anyway. Even if the quality was questionable, I didn't want to fight with a stomach full of the jagged leaves from earlier. "I don't care what sort of sad backstory Barney can come up with. Diana didn't use her magic on me just so I could put on a show for these dwarves."

"And I hope you can pull the upset somehow, Abyss-boy," the janitor said as he turned the cart around and moved toward the crowd of masked dwarves. He really did seem to take his work seriously, as listless as he looked. As I ate, I saw that Latis still held his own against Barney's disjointed kicks and punches. If I could describe it, the pineapple-headed boy's fighting style was most similar to Capoeira, as if he was mixing deceptive dance moves with his sweeps and kicks. It would be as difficult as fighting against Simon, even without teleportation magic.

I then remembered that the scars on my right arm hadn't fully healed either. It was still hard to keep a clenched right fist and throw a proper punch. I chewed on the fried rat and waffles anxiously, hoping that I would pack enough protein and calories to sprout another set of octopus tentacles when I needed it most. I still wondered if I could sneak out and disappear somehow and confront the God of Fire without fighting Barney. I didn't want to leave Latis behind, but Diana was a higher priority anyway. I would finish my current meal quickly and sneak out among the crowd of masked dwarves . . .

"All filled up now, are we?" Barney jumped out of the ring he was fighting in and landed on my side, a puff of smoke and flames appearing where his feet were. "Good, now the main spectacle can begin!" The masked dwarves cheered upon hearing that decree, and with two hands, Barney grabbed me by the waist and tossed me into the boxing ring.

"Abyss . . ." Latis frowned as I stumbled to my feet. "This is pretty bad. Barney's pretty strong when it comes to one-on-one, but when it comes to one-on-two, he's practically unbeatable." I wasn't sure if I'd misheard Latis, and the spiky-haired boy brushed off some dirt on his clothes. "But I should commend you for getting this far, even if Diana had to carry you."

"It really wasn't . . ." I turned back to Barney, who was waving his arms and pumping up the crowd. "Do I really have to fight here?"

"Just do your best to stay out of my way," Latis said. Barney jumped back into the ring and did a quick break-dancing move. He slid his legs around before he sprung back up to a fighting position.

"No matter how skilled you are as a fighter, Latis," Barney said. "Two knives and kicks won't do for the entertainment that this crowd truly desires. Most warriors can only manifest their skills through such limited means, caged by their own weapons. But I heard Abyss is different here . . ."

"Don't bite on his trap, Abyss," Latis said. "We'll have a better chance if we face him one-on-one."

Barney looked at me from the corner of his eye. "Your friend isn't entirely lying, but you wouldn't be so callous to let him die to me just to increase your chances of victory, would you?"

Chapter Four

"Barney's too fast as always!" One of the masked dwarves cheered.

Even after the short break, Latis still found himself in an uphill battle when it came to fighting Barney. No matter how he adjusted his knives, reversing his grip or going for cheap stabs, Barney's staggered rhythm in his Capoeira would keep him at bay with a fierce array of kicks. I tried to look for some hidden music or beat that would make it more predictable, but the enhanced snout I had once used refused to return to me.

Barney landed a powerful kick right into Latis' face within half a minute, and as Latis somersaulted backward to cushion the impact, Barney turned toward me with a curious eye. "He can put up a tough front all he wants, but it'll only take two or three more good kicks for me to deliver a fatal blow."

I looked back at Latis, who quickly swapped his knives and charged forth once again. Assuming that no one would drag him out of the ring, there was a good chance that Latis would die from his internal injuries before I could finish the fight against Barney.

But what did he mean that he was stronger one-on-two than one-on-one? Did his power automatically increase whenever a second opponent would fight him?

Latis' knives seemed to come closer this time, but it appeared that Barney was just baiting him. He was wobbling and swaying as he safely jabbed with his legs.

It was frustrating to watch. I turned back to Inder, and she only showed concern, unsure of what strategy I should actually use here. Worst-case scenario would be Barney's one-on-two skills completely destroy us, and Latis would curse my recklessness as I croaked. Helping Latis was never going to be as appealing as saving Inder or Diana, but could I really call myself a hero if I just waited several minutes and watched him fall?

"We'll take him together," I told Latis. "If we just mix it up and be unpredictable . . ."

Latis jumped back upon hearing my suggestion, and Barney pursued with a barrage of three kicks. "Abyss, don't . . ." It certainly looked like the fourth and fifth kicks would crush Latis' nose and smash out an eye. I rushed forward, only enchanting my feet with cat claws. As long as I remained cautious . . .

"*Aaagh*!" I only saw a couple of frames of sudden movement from Barney before pain shot through my injured right arm. I hadn't even thrown a punch yet. And why did I feel blood trickling down my left abdomen? Latis had collided with me and easily blocked my forced punch with his left arm, but his own forced stab had just luckily missed popping a hole in my organs. The crowd of masked dwarves cheered in excitement upon witnessing Barney's signature move, and as I got to my feet, I saw that the pineapple-headed boy had a slight smile on his face.

"I knew you would try it. And you'll probably try it again, given your foolhardiness," Barney said. His shoulders looked broader, and he had lost a button on his sleeveless shirt, which exposed his chiseled abs. "But seeing you wallow in despair while deciding whether or not to sacrifice your friend . . . that's the spectacle we will give to the crowd!"

"Abyss, just let me lose first," Latis insisted. "You won't get so lucky the next time he forces us to collide. Your odds of pulling a stunt like you did against Simon in the coliseum are far greater than overcoming his one-on-two techniques."

"If he's using magic, we can crack it somehow," I said. "There's a moment before he pulls off this technique, and if I can just time it . . ." Before I could finish my sentence, Latis was forced into defense and was blocking and dodging Barney's long, disjointed kicks. Had my memory just been wiped of the split second Barney had forced us against each other? Maybe he'd stopped time, but it definitely didn't seem like that. I could almost swear that I hadn't been *forced* to forget his technique, but rather, Barney had *persuaded* both of us to turn against each other . . .

"It appears our young hero is too afraid of receiving new holes in his belly!" Barney declared as he caught Latis in the chest with another powerful spinning kick. "So we shall let the first Child of Ice fall! Such is our victory, the feast for the flames!" The masked dwarves were split upon this decision and apparently wanted me to continue playing the role of a fool.

Holes in my belly certainly sounded painful. Barney slowed down his movements and jabs while he waited for Latis to catch his breath. So that was a prerequisite for his technique then? The first time, I charged in recklessly while only halfway balanced within my sprint. At the same time, I had to sell my intentions if I wanted to force Barney to reveal his hand.

"Not again, Abyss!" Latis warned as I ran forward to double-team Barney. Latis managed to turn and drop a knife this time, but I could see that his left arm was pulsing with Barney's red psionic magic. And I could see that he'd swiftly managed to grab onto my right arm again as time seemed to slow. He couldn't control our entire minds with this technique, or rather, he didn't want to. He wanted to influence us enough just so that we would look foolish, so foolish that we wouldn't be able to control what happened . . .

The masked dwarves around us began to swirl into exaggerated, wrinkly faces of hilarity and twisted glee. Latis' knife came closer and closer to piercing my abdomen, and that was when I would normally panic and grant Barney the humor he desired. But if I didn't dodge at all, it would also be a foolish end befitting of mockery. It was the better choice, however. I could take some of the blow with my Diamorph transformation, and as long as we looked foolish enough, Barney would stop his movements and magic to laugh at us.

"Diamorph *blubber* . . ." I whispered underneath my breath as the cells in my chest and abdomen began to shift. It would be comical for me to balloon up like an elephant seal, and taking the knife strike would still be painful, but it wouldn't be lethal. As I felt the cold metal blade pierce my new blubber armor, I turned and saw Barney caught up in the mood. He was letting his guard down just enough for the sole purpose of mocking us.

Moving was harder than it should have been. A large part of me wanted to succumb to Barney's magic and forget about my plans for a sneak attack. It was as if I was sent back to the third grade, and the cool, athletic kids were picking on me—this was part of Barney's trick, to weaken his opponents by reducing them to children. As if his Capoeira really wasn't enough . . .

Look even more foolish, I reminded myself.

Stumble toward Barney like an idiot while fifty pounds of fat weigh you down. Get him to laugh so that his face is wide open, and make him laugh even more with your busted arm.

Barney had expected me to throw a weak punch or fall over while I stumbled, but instead, I transformed my left knee into a diamond bludgeon and shot it toward his chest. It was a clean connection, but the momentum still forced me to fall over onto my side.

"Wahahahahaha!" The crowd of masked dwarves enjoyed the spectacle, nevertheless, even as their champion keeled over from the knee strike I'd landed.

"Aheh . . ." Barney chuckled as he stumbled backward. "Aheheahehehe!" *A madman, huh?* He served as a fitting preview for the insane God of Fire. "So you manage to fight against the embarrassment and even embraced it, Abyss-boy! Now I can see why Father was so interested in you."

I sighed as I gathered the blubber on my belly and tried to force my muscles to at least distribute it evenly.

"So then?" I asked. "Can you let Latis go, and can I face the God of Fire now?"

Barney chuckled. "Unfortunately, we have no choice but to fight to the end. The diamond blade that you need to seal Father is right here." Barney patted his belly. "And it'll take more than a few of those knee strikes to make me cough it up for you. In fact, I was forced to be a literal ball, tossed and passed between my older siblings. You mortals love to play games with balls, don't you?"

Latis walked up to my side. "I'm still against repeating this strategy, Abyss. Even if it does work, executing it will drive you insane."

I shrugged. "I'm still hoping we can talk this out, Barney. Even if we're talking about a god, we can work together and fight . . ."

"Heroes are good at scoring the ball, blocking the ball! But they will never be the ball!" Barney broke into his swift Capoeira motions, but this time, he was coming at me. "Right now, I see two perfect balls for me to juggle and dribble!"

Thwonk.

I was glad that I was covered in the protective suit of blubber, for my ribcage would definitely have been broken and scrambled if I took the blunt of Barney's kicks. My attempts to retaliate were easily dodged, however, and even though Barney was laughing, making him use his special technique was the only way to lower his guard. It was as if he was a fisherman playing with a helpless pufferfish before throwing him back into the ocean.

"I can play with this ball for hours, maybe even days, Child of Ice!" Barney declared. "But after he croaks, your death will come shortly after! Will you abandon him just to live a little longer?" I could sense that Barney was getting more and more aggressive with his kicks. At this rate, even if he couldn't simply smash my bones, putting enormous force and pressure against my blubber shield would cause a dangerous amount of internal bleeding.

Latis finally decided that he had to bail me out again and came at Barney from behind. This would again trigger his special technique, and as I prepared to be publicly humiliated, I entered the mysterious world of Barney's memories. Even if I bit against the embarrassment with stoic conviction, Barney would insist that I come face-to-face with his past.

What I saw made the beating that I'd just taken look like a stubbed toe. Barney was, as he described, literally being forced into a crunched-up position, being juggled between two other children, and served as an all-purpose sports ball. "Father chose to interfere with humans for many reasons," Barney explained. "One reason was because of their capacity for humor, whether it stemmed from random bouts of creativity or savage insults and mockery. It was fascinating to him how man could be such a serious creature to work from dawn to dusk for harvesting and crafting, but be so utterly destructive and foolish to destroy and pillage in drunken rampages. It wasn't that man was a perfect embodiment of chaos, but rather a perfect transition from order to chaos that continued to be captured and reproduced in art and history."

"But things go from chaos to order, as well," I said as I snapped from Barney's memories. Another one of Latis' knife strikes was starting to pierce my belly. "I can only see a fraction of what you were forced into, Barney, but . . ."

"But what?" Barney laughed at my suggestion as if he

found it extremely predictable. "No amount of order can even bring a fraction of the delight that nonsense and chaos can. No matter what field, your species has embraced the *useless* when it comes to sports, literature, or the arts. And even the language that rolls under our tongues is constantly evolving into different accents and dialects. It was you who chose to remain a hero and stay within this world of chaos. Even if you seal my father with the diamond blade, you're only preferring one brand of chaos to another. And all for what? What has been truly saved?"

The laughter from the crowd hit harder this time. *What could I truly save?* Even if people weren't forced to be literal balls, there was no way to keep the strong from picking on the weak or even prevent the whims of fate, chance, and luck, when it came to success. Just as humans laughed at cats and dogs and monkeys, I was perhaps, at best, a mere spectacle for these higher powers . . .

I thought of Diana and even my pathetic attempts to save Moka from Oljatu. It was the same farce, acting on instinct and goodwill without any guarantee of a decent result. And Barney expected me to continue putting up a fight. It didn't matter if he won or lost. He was a mere agent of this God of Fire. Just as humans turned other species into food products, pets, and laboratory experiments, humanity would always be one step behind these higher powers. I would save myself the pain if I just let Latis' knife catch a vital organ, and many animals gave up kicking and thrashing as they were eaten alive.

And again, the sensation of thousands of hungry teeth and enraged shrieks dug into my limbs, and it was enough for me to turn toward Barney. This time, the pineapple-headed boy didn't keep his guard up, for he was both amused by my grit and curious on how hard I could hit him. Without thinking of my injury, I threw the hardest right punch I could muster, and upon contact with Barney's face, I collapsed to the ground in pain. I cursed the inconsistency of my Diamorph powers and my failure to heal a simple wound.

"So this is the next bearer of For One's Glory." I suddenly heard a foreign voice in my head. Time stopped in the boxing arena, and now I was in an ancient palace, face-to-face with a muscular Pharaoh on his throne. "I was upset that Drsyna had taken the power that I was promised, but perhaps you are the one who is most fit to wield it. You contracted with the legendary Witch, after all."

"For One's what?" I wondered curiously.

"Even if your Diamorph transformation was enough to get you through your quests, using it as much as you do will drive you insane," the Pharaoh replied. His face was slightly familiar, and I remembered him from the first dream I had after eating the impala with Diana. "It took thousands of years for her to make another hero to bless—and curse. Hopefully, you will be the hero to end all heroes, Abyss."

I remembered how grueling the fights with Grigory had been, and I knew that if I went head-to-head with the Pharaoh here, it wouldn't end well. But I also remembered how ruthless Grigory's allies were in the judgment of modern humans, having turned them into tools for this Pharaoh's great purpose. "I'm not interested in being one of your servants. You, Oljatu, and the God of Fire should all leave . . ."

"Be grateful for my blessings, Abyss," the Pharaoh said firmly. "If it hadn't been for my efforts, most humans would be plowing the fields from dawn to dusk or be subject to the whims of spears and arrows in ancient warfare. It is because of the contracts I signed long ago that you've been able to play hero . . . both in your books and video games and in your current quest."

I sighed, too tired to attempt to outsmart him, let alone engage in a physical fight. "Tell me about the power that I got from Diana. She used it to save me and shoot down the God of Fire in the room with five suns, right?"

"It's rather difficult to explain, but I can tell you that it requires sacrifice," the Pharaoh replied. "Something that you haven't been able to do so far with your desire to save everyone."

"Well, yeah," I said. "That's what heroes do, even if the odds seem grim . . ."

"Right now, you're only managing to stay in this fight by the use of that power," the Pharaoh continued. "Heroes are supposed to save things, but they also must destroy. Together, we will destroy humanity's follies, its gluttony and sloth and aimless lust. And I will teach you how to properly perform your first sacrifice . . ."

Time was still frozen in the midst of the boxing match, and as predictable as it might seem, I saw Latis' essence and energy flow toward my body. "So, in order to win this fight, I have to sacrifice Latis?" Even if I hadn't gotten along too well with the spiky-headed Child of Ice, I couldn't betray him just for power.

"He's a sacrifice anyways, an irrational agent produced by the essence of order and stability, the God of Ice," the Pharaoh responded. "By using your power, you're condemning him to a certain fate. He will live after this battle, however."

"Wait a minute . . ." Just as I wanted to protest and ask more questions, Barney's spinning kicks caught me straight in the chest. More and more of my blubber armor was being painted purple and red.

Was this the amount of support the Pharaoh could give me, or did he expect me to make my own decision?

"Like a true amateur, your right straight is your strongest move," Barney said, observing as he finished off his kick combo with a powerful leg sweep that sent me toppling onto my back. "But with the power you've awakened, your odds of beating me aren't so slim, after all."

I stumbled to my feet and realized that my blubber armor

was shrinking. The bruises that had previously been soaked up by the mysterious fat were now working their way and pressing against my vital organs.

"So I'm here to be a sacrifice?" Latis asked. Barney turned to him and decided to switch targets once again, and when Latis tried to block with his knives and kicks, he looked even slower than before.

"Better a sacrifice than the ball, then a mindless slave!" Barney declared. "Humanity loves sacrifices! But young Abyss, do you love humanity?"

I wondered what fate I would exactly condemn Latis to and whether or not it was worse than death in battle. Barney was both prepared for me to rush in and prepared to outright kill Latis with a lethal kick.

"Abyss, don't mind me!" Latis said. "If you really acquired that power from Diana . . . from Sobekhotep, rather, I'll make whatever sacrifice it demands!"

That was enough for me to snap out of my indecision, and as I rushed forward to intercept Barney's barrage of kicks and spins, I pumped up my heartrate and felt Latis' energy and essence drift toward me. As Barney performed his technique, setting up Latis and me for another awkward collision, this time, I saw additional imagery, even if I didn't see the Pharaoh.

Before Shakespeare, even before the *Iliad* and the *Odyssey*, humanity was tested again and again. Beyond the quests for food and water, soldiers and warriors died in the thousands when kingdoms warred and raiders pillaged. Oljatu wanted me to become a fine conqueror, but if I was to be a hero, I at least had to be a survivor.

Did so many die so that a few heroes could live? Was modern man too sheltered to realize this when their heroes and adventurers survived each coming battle?

I suddenly saw orange flames swirl around Latis' body—or rather, his future self in the fate I'd condemned him to.

"For One's Glory," I said to myself. This time, I was moving swifter and was putting the remaining energy I had into reinforcing the knuckles on my right fist. I didn't have time to think of an unpredictable move, but I knew that Barney would leave his guard down for just long enough. I sent another right straight at Barney, and this one should have crushed his skull.

"Wahahahahha!" Barney confidently laughed as he grabbed onto my wrist with his left hand. "As humor has begun to fade with your stale and worn tomfoolery, I have just enough to make the fight last longer . . ." Barney was already turning into his next move, and this time, I knew he was kicking at his full strength. His ankle would have crushed my neck had I not blocked it with my left forearm, but now, Barney was preparing another attack. This one came much lower, and I could only block it with my right arm.

Barney may have been half-insane, but he knew how to wear his opponents down. I wouldn't be able to do anything with my crippled right arm for a few more seconds, while I could probably punch at half-strength with my left. He even gloated a bit and did a useless twirling move before preparing his next kick.

I still had both of my legs, but I couldn't muster making enough muscle to do the kangaroo kick.

So what if you can't punch? I was hearing my own voice combined with Latis' now. I would never be able to master a true martial arts technique, but with For One's Glory, I found my best current option.

Just a small movement with my legs was enough. Barney was aiming for my head with a sweeping kick, bringing himself close enough so that I could reach him with my elbows. Pushing off my right leg, I smashed my left elbow into his stomach and managed to score a clean hit.

Barney tumbled backward in shock and began to choke,

and a large lump was beginning to form in his throat. "Wahahaha!" he was still laughing in the midst of it, and the crowd of masked dwarves was cheering upon witnessing the dramatic upset. "Wa—kofff, ukoffuwah!"

Clink-clan-kuu!

The familiar diamond blade that I'd unearthed was forced out of Barney's throat and spun along the boxing ring. I sighed in relief, picked up the blade, and ignored the saliva and stomach acid as best as I could. "I wish I had brought a sheath, as well . . ." I said as I brought it close to my belt. The diamond blade unexpectedly formed its own hooks and strapped itself at my waist.

"Very few can wield that blade," Barney said as he struggled to his feet. I noticed that the outlines of his body were beginning to turn into steam and wispy clouds of orange gas. "Now that you have the blade, I won't be able to maintain this form. Perhaps Father meant you to come here so that he could laugh at me, rather than bring me here so that I could test you." It didn't feel like I had truly won this battle, just like it had been with Grigory.

"Are you really going to go back to . . . being a ball, though?" I asked.

"As long as humans are playing with balls, I'll be a ball," Barney said, now with half of his face dissolved. "Don't look at me like you want to save me, hero. Pick your battles better. Otherwise, it's a waste of that talent . . ." With that said, Barney faded into wisps of pure energy. The ground and walls shook as a pathway toward another hall began to open. Hopefully, it wouldn't be much longer until we reached the God of Fire.

"Cursed with the diamond blade, but also blessed with For One's Glory," Latis said as he stumbled toward me. He still looked as if he was trying to shake off a bad nightmare, aware that I had just condemned him to an unpleasant fate. "Nice elbow there. Of course, your cat feet helped generate the force you needed. But . . ." Inder and Diana walked toward the boxing ring and quickly undid the chains that blocked off our exit. "I don't think I'll be able to help with your final battle."

"If you're that beat up from fighting against Barney, you'll definitely need my help when it comes to fighting the God of Fire," Diana said. It appeared that the spell Barney had cast on her had worn off, and now she was back to her usual personality.

"I saw him . . . the Pharaoh, the one you'd worked for," I began. "What exactly did you do to save me within that room with five suns?"

"It's something that I'll probably regret," Diana said. "Assuming you manage to complete this quest, I'll have to stick around with you. And as you use For One's Glory more and more, the pain . . . mental, as well as physical . . . will increase as you bear many people's hopes and dreams, regrets and curses. But if he really bothered to grant you a face-to-face audience . . ." Diana's voice trailed off, and she sighed. "It's going to be more than just a hostage situation like it was with Grigory. I've known for quite some time to not try to outwit Sobekhotep."

"And this blade?" I asked, grabbing the hilt with my injured right hand. I'd never practiced using my left hand much, from basketball to writing, and was hoping that the blade would auto-pilot me once again.

"It takes a high degree of skill to use that blade," Latis said. "Many say the will of the original wielder still resides there, and if you can't wield it properly . . . well, best-case scenario, your arm gets ripped off. Worst-case, the blade decides to mince you into pieces."

"That's not how it's supposed to work. I'm supposed to pull the blade from a pedestal or just be good at it when I pick it up like in fantasy novels," I grumbled. "The God of Ice helped calm the waters enough for us to get to this dungeon, but I wonder if he's willing to help us in the final battle, as well."

Just as Latis was beginning to say something, the ceiling and ground began to rumble, and the four of us headed toward the new hallway that had opened when I'd defeated Barney. As I ran, I felt the injuries I had accumulated begin to pile up on my arms and body. It was no problem in video games when it came to getting to the final boss with only a few hearts remaining, but at this stage, I doubted I could fight half as well as I did against Barney. Diana noticed my weariness and clapped me on the back.

"Choose when you sync with me carefully," she said. "Inder helped reinforce them, but I still only have one powerful arrow left. She gave me two more fragile ice arrows that will slow the God of Fire down for a couple of seconds at best."

"Easier said than done," I replied. "If I'm too careful, I'll just run out of stamina in the middle of the fight." As we ran down the hallways, the corridor seemed to twist and turn. The walls were spinning as if the whole world was the dream of a drunken architect. "The God of Fire makes no sense. I feel like we would have been defeated if he was serious about this, but if his main goal was for me to beat Barney, is he now doing this just to make me suffer?"

"Good question," an unexpected voice answered me. I had expected another crowd of masked dwarves, but this time there were only three spectators—or maybe two and a half, to be precise. Oljatu, the old khan who had wanted me to succeed his tribe, had been the first to speak. "No matter what's in store for the future, you certainly are progressing a bit too slowly."

I tensed up and remembered how I had run away from our duel a few days ago. "I've got no time to fight you, as well, Oljatu," I said.

"I'm merely here to observe your performance," Oljatu

said. "Perhaps you're destined to expand your horizons beyond our tribe. But you won't get far as a hero trying to save everybody." The other person who had been summoned here was Sonny, the mixed-race boy who had taught me the basics of boxing. And next to him was a glossy crystal ball. From within, I could see Dorothy's bright pink hair and smirking face.

"I'm glad you made it all the way here!" Dorothy cheered. "I thought you might need an extra sacrifice, so I brought an old friend along. Even if you don't use him, I'm sure you'll put up a much cooler fight than boring old Simon would!"

"So we're fighting after all, aren't we?" Diana stayed close to me while Inder and Latis joined Sonny, Oljatu, and Dorothy. "I wonder if I could just sacrifice Oljatu first . . ."

"If you were to try to abuse that new power you gained, you would crush yourself with too many burdens," the God of Fire finally spoke up, and when he initiated the conversation, dozens of icy mirrors sprouted across the room. It reminded me of the time when the God of Ice had approached me in the stormy seas. No, this was definitely the same brand of power. "You have many questions, do you not? I can lie and make a comfortable answer, or I can try to tell the truth. But I never contained myself with your human intents, limited in your endeavors."

Finally the God of Fire manifested his physical body. He was golden brown and muscular, with black and blue tattoos constantly swirling and shifting in random patterns on his shirtless upper half. He sprouted two additional spiny appendages from his back, which carried a fresh swirl of blue flames at their ends. "I'm feeling creative with my name. Pick a letter, please, Abyss . . ."

"Okay . . ." I started.

"*K*! Kraken, cracking cuisine . . ." Even while manifesting a human body, he was as insane as I had ever expected, clutching his forehead as he rattled his brain for syllables. "End of the alphabet? Z! I shall be called Krakazrlr for today!"

"I'm pretty beat up after the fight with Barney," I admitted. "Since we already got so far in the dungeon, can I just seal you with this blade and be done with it . . ."

"Humans! Always so picky and petty! When happiness comes, they must subject themselves to more standards, bizarre and reckless as they come!" Krakazrlr began. "It should be enough, right? You had your journey as a hero, so why seal me with that wretched blade and subject yourself to more pain? Why not simply dance in the fields of chaos because that is all you humans are good for! That is the role of all intelligent beings . . . to increase the possibilities of chaos and nonsense! Or could you, would you escape into some partial understanding of eternity, hunched over test tubes and particle accelerators?"

Krakazrlr did a triple backflip and broke into a wild breakdance as he jumped about the mirrors. His two flaming appendages worked like supernatural tails. I could tell that he wasn't quite teleporting like Simon, but he could cover a few meters in a split second, thanks to his additional limbs.

"Will it ever be enough chaos for you to stop bombarding heroes with . . . with mindless chaos?" I asked, remembering how bizarre my journey had been.

"Not until humanity regresses to the sentience of a wild boar!" Krakazrlr insisted. "Why struggle so, Abyss? Whether your end comes in youth or old age, new heroes will pick up the torch. I promise if you work for me, you'll have a better position than the janitor, and you won't be juggled about like Barney . . ."

I was getting dizzy and wobbly just by listening to the God of Fire rant. "Negotiations are over then!" I said as I brandished the diamond blade. I remembered how conveniently it had fought for me during my first battle against Melosh, but this time, spines sprouted from the hilt and started digging themselves deep into my forearm. I could hear the thoughts of the previous bearer, and my vision almost blackened at the swarm of negativity.

I shouldn't have been the next in line to wield this sword, but . . .

"I'm going to see this legendary Witch that contracted with me, at least! I don't care if she's as crazy as Dorothy!"

"The Witch . . . the Pharaoh, both are mindless, cursed pursuits compared to the sheer joy of chaos!" Krakazrlr was suddenly in front of me and was attacking with his two flaming appendages. They were turned into stabbing weapons like a scorpion's tail.

The diamond blade automatically helped me block the strikes, but I had to quickly move my body and legs to prevent my arm from being pulled out of my socket. "You've got effort, but little else . . ."

Perhaps I had picked up on enough attack patterns from the fight against Barney, but I barely got my left arm up in time to block his powerful hammer-fist. Now Krakazrlr was striking with his two flaming appendages while he played the part of an aggressive boxer toying with his prey. There was no way to counterattack without dropping my guard somewhere—but the sword that had almost merged with my right arm insisted on protecting me from harm's way, on fighting with finesse.

"Effort . . . and just enough foolishness to drive even you mad, Krakazrlr!"

Even if it was just for a split second, I got the diamond blade to stand down just enough to make a reckless charge forward. I guarded my neck and head with my left arm while I sprinted forward with my familiar cat's feet, ready to take at least two severe burns from the flaming appendages.

"I like your style, kid!" Krakazrlr exclaimed as I swooped in with an upward slash just as his flaming appendages connected.

"*Aaarrrrgh*!" I stumbled in pain as I fell to one knee and balanced myself by planting the diamond blade within the ground. It was a good thing I'd covered my head, for the entirety of my left forearm was now covered in burn scars. The whip-like appendage had also landed on my left ankle and ripped off the skin from the back to expose the muscles beneath.

"Your work with the blade . . . the Pharaoh would definitely approve of you!" Krakazrlr explained as he jumped backward, a giant, glowing scar having formed on his chest. "Oh, careful, careless. Which one should I choose?"

"Diana!" I turned to the cheetah-cheeked hunter, who had already drawn her bow. "I'll need you somehow . . . some way . . ."

"I can hardly track his movements!" Diana replied. "And since you're struggling so much to handle the blade, I can't properly sync with you either . . ."

"If the world's too hot, too cold, and space too dark and glum, show old Krakky here that you're greater than the sums . . ." the God of Fire sang as he swung about the multiple ice mirrors.

"Abyss!" Inder shouted out. "Go to the mirrors! It's your only chance of winning this battle!"

I turned back to Diana, but I had no time to confirm whether or not it was the optimal strategy as I barely dodged two deadly sweeps of flaming appendages. My left ankle hurt when I put weight on it, so I could really only dodge by rolling and stumbling about. I had one good limb at best, and I felt if I pushed myself to block with my left arm again, the searing heat would completely destroy all of the remaining nerve endings there.

"Oh, pity this age of princesses! Oh, joy to be wild! Forget your place to save a young lass, of romance, summer's child." Krakazrlr slowed his attacks just enough to find a matching rhyme, and I struggled to focus and gain control of the diamond blade I held. "For truly man does yet belong, but he will often claim it wrong, to war and power in the empire of grass!"

"Don't lose, Abyss!" Oljatu yelled suddenly. "You have unfinished business!"

Krakazrlr's main body was too far away to strike without forcing my body to sustain another injury. *But if I could just change the angle enough so that a desperate block with my diamond blade becomes a . . .*

Krlsssh!

As I swung the diamond blade, it severed half of the appendage that had sprouted from Krakazrlr's back. Before I could capitalize on the opening, the God of Fire jumped back toward the hall of mirrors once more.

"It's our best option!" I said to Diana as I ran toward the icy mirrors that Krakazrlr was prancing around in. If Inder and Diana could help me just enough to let me deliver a decisive strike, the battle seemed winnable. I knew I wouldn't get very far by settling for attacking Krakazrlr's long appendages or by making narrow wounds in his chest.

"Oh, glistening, precious, gold and jewelry!" The God of Fire began to smash many of the mirrors and was probably trying to protect himself from Inder's trap before dealing with me. "To impress, is that her last tomfoolery? Perchance to value reason more than dreams, to be content and to never miss, to abandon your . . ." Mid-poem, Krakazrlr shot at me with his two appendages. The one that I'd severed moved much slower and was now slow enough to leave to my injured left arm. "Oh, bliss that glistens! Oh, joy that be! To always grant us heroes, it seems?"

Just focus enough for Diana and Inder, I thought to myself as I remembered how I'd helped her shoot down the target in the Field of Five Suns.

Empty just enough of my mind for her . . .

"Ohoho! That's a close one!" Krakazrlr flipped up and over a powerful ice arrow that whizzed past his head, resuming his wild dance across the mirrors. "But you seem to have too many regrets, like anyone would have over the course of millennia! You've forgotten how to live, even when you're finally generous to give another hero a true chance. Two arrows left, are there not?"

"Sorry about that, Abyss!" Diana exclaimed. "I was almost there . . ."

"We'll worry about the Pharaoh later!" I said. "I'm not going to serve a poetic fruitcake that forces his own child to be a ball!"

"And yet you seek to preserve your current species! Out of no more than a matter of habit!"

I'd thought that I'd tuned out Krakazrlr by now, but his words were enough to make me hesitate. The diamond blade was now doing most of the work, and my right arm grew numb as I felt the tendons in my socket loosen. People usually ignored things that were too complex, be it scientific knowledge or philosophy, but I couldn't ignore the God of Fire.

"And what are you then? Chaos for the sake of chaos?" I questioned. Krakazrlr was unfazed by the question and continued his offensive arsenal.

"But man has desired and invited chaos . . . of without which he would be no more than a bundle of instincts, a predestined path. Put the blade down and join me, Abyss! You desired to be a hero, but you desired greater glory than fighting an evil villain."

Even if I was—no, even if people in general wanted more from the villain, they would still try their best to be a hero, as well. I somehow found more power in my injured left leg, and as I regained my footing, I managed to go on the offensive against the half-mad God of Fire. Krakazrlr blocked with his arms and back appendages, but I could tell that even my amateur swordsmanship was leaving scars and cuts. However, my right arm was still struggling to stay in its socket, and I would probably lose control of my feet before I could win the battle of attrition.

"Abyss!" Inder called from the sidelines. "He's moving inside of the mirrors! Make sure he doesn't sneak up on you!"

I jumped away from the Krakazrlr I was fighting and strained my Diamorph abilities to enhance my senses.

"Humans are pathetic creatures of habit, but once in a while, they impress." Krakazrlr's voice was now an echo. "With such refined machinery, they determine that within the universe I created, there's something more than nonsense. And they only determine that it's more meaninglessness, isn't it?"

Something clicked in my brain, and I fell on my behind from the sudden dizziness and confusion. All animal brains were determined to see things through space and time, but human beings could vaguely conceive of the idea of different laws through mathematics and theoretical physics.

But now I was seeing it!

Krakazrlr was inside one mirror, then six, then a dozen, and then none, and as he moved from mirror to mirror—were these just his reflections? It wasn't quite *movement* at all, but I would have to gamble . . .

The current universe didn't make sense, but there was one point in which nothing needed to be explained. The moment before the Big Bang where all was One—that would be the only essence, the first cause in which I could trace the footsteps of Krakazrlr and his true position. But witnessing that moment would be suicide for my pathetic primate brain, wouldn't it?

The mirrors were a gift from the God of Ice, giving me hints on how to restrain my enemy . . .

Crrkrkr!

I felt the bones in my arms pop as I viciously commanded my diamond blade to block my heart—it was distracted, confused by all of the different enemy positions it was encountering. My entire right arm was in a state of burning numbness, but it was preferable to being stabbed through the heart by Krakazrlr's two appendages. I could see nothing in front of me, but for this split second that was his true position, and . . .

Thokk!

Diana's enchanted ice arrow struck the God of Fire straight through the chest, and he laughed triumphantly in glee. "Well done, but it'll take quite a bit more than that, you see." Krakazrlr was no longer in his *cloudy* state full of wavy probabilities, and an arrow shaft was sprouting straight from his heart, having frozen a huge chunk of his upper body. "But do you have the strength to launch that last arrow of yours?" I turned and found that Diana had sunk to one knee, as syncing with me for her second shot had taken the life and breath out of her. "She's more of a fool than you! But fools are great, it's true!"

"Don't strain yourself, Diana!" I yelled. "That should be enough for me to finish him off!" I rushed forward with the diamond blade and aimed for a clean stab through Krakazrlr's chest. As I felt the blade make fresh contact, I thought the grueling battle was finally over, but instead, it had been another trap.

"I pulled off nothing fancy," the God of Fire explained as the diamond blade began to dissolve. I had managed to blow off Krakazrlr's left arm and one of his spiny appendages, but he was still a formidable foe with four limbs remaining. "It requires perfect discipline and commitment to perform the final seal on me. Deep down, part of you has doubts, Abyss. Part of you sees the value of the chaos I've brought to this world."

As I attempted to pull out the hilt of the diamond blade, I found that its jagged edges merely scraped at my palm. As I tried to ball it into a fist instead, I found that my right arm could only hang limp at my side. Both of my arms were injured now—maybe I could manifest enough energy for one crucial punch. "Well," I muttered to myself. "No one likes it when a story gets too predictable, right?"

"I can no longer traverse the mirrors, now bound to this corporeal body, but I gain strength from the billions of humans that yearn for me." Krakazrlr rushed forward, and as hard as I tried to block with my left arm, his punches and kicks left a fresh set of heavy bruises on my chest, and he finished it off with one final leg sweep. I toppled onto the ground and hard stone, and I was sure this would be over, but the God of Fire wanted me to hear a few more words.

"For most animals that evolve, pure instinct is enough for survival," Krakazrlr said sternly. "Out of trillions of life forms in the universe, few develop the capabilities to go beyond. Beyond to where, however? For you lot of primates needed language, needed tools to strategize and deceive. The God of Ice insists on eternity and truth, but why not examine the alternatives in deception?"

I stumbled to my feet. *Think, think . . .*

My only chance was to outwit this bizarre god.

Images started to flash in the icy mirrors, but instead of the God of Fire, I saw myself through decades, through early childhood and adulthood, and the thoughts and habits that came from my material body. The images quickly shifted to my classmates and then many variations of the eight billion people that lived in the world. The pattern was always the same when a child became an adult, and it wasn't particularly pretty. "So are adults really as boring as they appear?" I asked.

"Ever since the lot of you painted on caves and danced around a fire, you desired more," Krakazrlr said. "Priests and shamans promise the faithful salvation, while the materialistic indulge in what? Gambling with money, gambling with time in futile, artistic endeavors, although seemingly a little less futile with a proper dash of chaos . . ."

Pssshtk!

I was so lost in the mirror imagery that I didn't see Krakazrlr's fist ram into my face yet again. "Humans can be as dull as they are grim, but then you're not a god that I ought to follow . . . in fact, there's no origin that quite secures me!"

The world around me was spinning as I struggled to reopen my eyes. Oddly enough, however, the punch had given me new motivation and strength as I balled up my right fist.

The bruises all over my body started to fade away as I felt a new bolt of adrenaline. I knew I couldn't waste my one true punch too early, but all I had to do was secure his position enough for Diana to sync with me and land another critical hit. Krakazrlr insisted that the intelligent resort to his brand of chaos in order to escape meaninglessness, but meaninglessness could provide an opportunity for rebirth. Even if I had messed up with the diamond blade, even if I could see so many different versions of me—so many different failures in the hall of mirrors that tried to mock me, I was more than the sum of my parts. Somewhere deep through another mirror, I would be another *me* in the dozens of possible futures that had responded to chaos with some sort of understanding and order.

"Seeing you struggle is too much! Seeing her struggle is just as fine!" the God of Fire announced. "Struggle as you may, inevitable fate is to decay. To a god like me, it matters not, as in the end, chaos will be brought."

Was I walking into a trap that would be laid down months later, decades later?

As if my life and story were no more than a pile of *Jenga* blocks that were waiting to fall into pieces. Krakazrlr still blocked and countered my jabs with lighter punches. He was hitting me hard enough to hurt, but he always made sure that

I could continue fighting.

The universe seemed to be too large, too deadly, and too meaningless—but if nothing else, it was a hero's job to tell a story. A story would bring the chaos of the world down to a single point, just enough for a pathetic ape brain to see—or rather, just enough so that even a divine embodiment of chaos would seek to dwell in a true body. As Krakazrlr and I continued to trade blows, I forced myself to wait to give Diana the signal. The moment in which he decided to adapt a human brain, to turn chaos into order using flawed curiosity . . .

"Diamorph Tiger!" I put all of the black, glistening oil that swirled around my feet into the strongest punch I could muster. Even then, I knew it wasn't enough to break through Krakazrlr's defenses. Sometimes a hero couldn't look cool in his job, after all.

Instead, I felt myself stuck in the body of Diana. I could feel how much her right arm strained from pulling back the bowstring and how her entire body was lit ablaze by activating For One's Glory. My original body, in Abyss, had just had his strongest punch blocked by Krakazrlr's extended tail appendage, and in that split second where organic, biological material connected with a divine entity, the seal that had trapped the God of Fire began to activate. And all it needed was one good strike to redo the seal. It was a shame that I had lost the diamond blade, but Diana's arrow would have to do.

Thokk!

As the seal was hit dead-center by Diana's perfect marksmanship, the cheetah-cheeked archer fell to her knees in a daze, and my consciousness returned to my original body. "You have only delayed me with this weak seal. Or rather, was it your purpose all along, young Abyss?" Krakazrlr asked as his body began to dissolve into spheres of light and flickers of flame. "For enough chaos is needed for the Pharaoh to rise and perform, but I hope you become more than a slave of the Order, Abyss!"

I sunk to my knees in exhaustion. After a few seconds, Krakazrlr's body dissolved completely, and my next priority was turning toward Diana. But by now, I didn't have enough strength to make it to where she was, let alone carry her. The icy mirrors disappeared into smoke and steam, and I continued to feel my muscles relax. I felt as if the God of Fire had managed to pull off a small victory. My mind was going back to those mushroom hallucinations, where Inder's chest turned into rolling clouds of flesh . . .

No, something else was rolling toward me, along with the sound of two pairs of footsteps. "So this is where we part for now," Oljatu said as he leaned over me. "I could only watch through Dorothy's crystal, but you're making progress, my descendant." Like the God of Fire, my distant ancestor was also fading into smoke and wisps. "Perhaps the Pharaoh's rising will allow me an extended stay in this time period. Or perhaps Dorothy would be generous enough to bring me back as well . . ."

"Maybe I'll let you out again if I get too sloppy," Dorothy suggested. "It was my job to seal the aether rifts when Abyss pulled out the diamond blade, and Oljatu managed to sneak out. You put up a much better fight than Simon would have, although, on the other hand . . . Simon would have properly sealed the God of Fire with the diamond blade."

"Thanks for not using me as a sacrifice," Sonny said. "Even if the rest of the heroes and clerics would have Simon take over your quest instead, I think you had the right to carry out the terms of your contract." Sonny lent me a hand and helped me get to my feet.

"Diana . . . For One's Glory . . ." I muttered, still not convinced that we'd finished the sync after my final fight. "I don't really care about the partial seal, but rather . . ." As I turned, I saw that Inder and Latis were tending to the cheetah-cheeked archer.

"I also had a dream of that Pharaoh," Sonny tried to begin. "And I usually don't get hero dreams. I don't remember it well. Maybe one of my ancestors had served in his army and made a pact millennia ago."

"Sorry to drag you into more weird things then," I said. "I'm guessing back to the Western Sanctuary . . . *ukoff*!" A blob of glowing, silver fluid left my throat and splattered onto the ground. "I'm guessing it's back to the Western Sanctuary?"

A quick *fwoom* hit my ears, and I saw a girl with spiky red hair enter the arena. "So the contracted hero only made a partial seal. Looks like this is more work for Fayria, stuck in this form, is she. But hey, our ball is back, right, Starkov?" Now that I thought of it, this girl had a striking resemblance to Barney.

"And our ball tried his best to be a real boy." Another *fwoom* of flames, and now a tall boy with curly red hair appeared next to the girl. I really wasn't in the shape to fight, especially after throwing up silver liquid. The boy quickly observed my puke. "Fayria refers to herself in third person. Starkov here. I am Starkov," the boy said. "We'd better get this half-baked hero . . . and the bearer of For One's Glory . . . back into the mortal realm before he barfs up more quicksilver." As if on cue, my stomach rumbled again, and another blob of silver fluid made its way up my throat and out onto the rocky floor.

"The mortal realm?" I asked. "Will the monsters and weirdoes of the world really just let me recover for weeks, even months . . . *ukoff*!" Now that I thought of it, I'd tried my best not to get homesick, but there were so many simple things I missed. Starkov looked at Sonny and the crystal ball that was trailing behind us.

"You'll be lucky to recover for a few months at best," Starkov said. He pulled something out of his pocket and tossed a couple of chocolate *Pocky* sticks into his mouth. "Curse this human form. Always so hungry and thirsty and whatnot . . ."

"You're worried about your guide, aren't you?" Fayria said. "It's hard to imagine that she decided to use her greatest power for a reckless boy like you. She will also have to integrate into your mortal realm and regularly sync with your body in order to prevent you from degenerating."

"Will everybody be all right?" I asked. "With Melosh and the clerics, wouldn't they use Simon's absence to wipe out us heroes for good?" I remembered how he'd agreed upon the ceasefire at the coliseum.

"He was ready to target Simon specifically to weaken the heroes," Starkov answered. "But he seems to have a different opinion regarding you. In addition, as you've met that man from the Moving Restaurant, there exists dissent between the priests and clerics regarding whether or not Witches should really be hunted down."

"And what about you, Inder? Latis?" I asked. Even if the bond of trust and friendship between us seemed underdeveloped, Latis had allowed himself to be sacrificed down the stretch, and Inder had done something with the hall of mirrors in the final battle.

"We'll see each other again someday," Inder suggested. "Although Father . . . the God of Ice, definitely would have preferred it if we properly sealed the God of Fire."

"Well, that's not your fault," I said. "I only had a few minutes to try to learn how to use the blade . . ." My stomach rumbled once again, and this time, I felt the silver fluid travel through my bones and veins. It was eating and chewing away at my right arm. My fingers were wriggling and snapping like drunken worms, and as I tried to grab onto my wrist and stabilize, I keeled over and fell onto my back.

"It looks like we'll have to fast-travel out of here," Starkov said as he ran over to the trailing crystal ball and held it up to his face. "Dorothy . . ."

"Oh? Teleporting through the dungeon is quite some work, even for a Witch of my caliber," Dorothy said from the crystal's inside. "You better give me some overrides and maybe a delicious cake for my efforts." White flames and energy surrounded the crystal ball, and before I knew it, the world began to spin once more. It was the same sensation that I'd gone through when I'd clung onto Simon with my tentacles, except for dozens of times stronger.

As much as I wanted to return to a peaceful life, I also knew that this would be one of my few opportunities to look for answers. While floating in the sea of aether, I could see through past and future. I could see the remnants, the faint trails of the magic that I'd been granted through the contract with my Witch. Even if the God of Fire and Ice could never be understood by the human brain, I wanted an explanation, or at least instructions and warnings regarding my powers.

"Hush," a new female voice said. I was now face-to-face with my patron Witch, although the left half of her body was shrouded in a cloud of what appeared to be cherry blossoms. She was wearing a black dress and a crown of black crystals, and behind her were twisted pieces of modern art, of exaggerated, wrinkly faces, and flesh bits. I tried to speak, but I realized that my voice came out in a series of animalistic growls. "You are limited in my presence, so I couldn't meet you. I can only try to answer some of your questions, young Abyss.

"Why choose at all when it comes to heroes?" My patron Witch sighed. "Is it enough to flip the coin and roll the dice? Many Witches decide to choose heroes with promise and who are likely to overcome insurmountable odds. But that was never what I thought a hero needed. Why, I would rather see a hero with the possibility for *despair*. To despair enough is to transform enough, in the void of death and nothingness, and to truly allow the world to be reborn."

So was she just as insane as Dorothy and the God of Fire? Or had my power taken a life of its own ever since the first fight with Grigory?

"You haven't faced a fraction of your own potential despair, but it's also about me as well, you see. Outside the known universe, infinite possibilities exist, you know. A world where I didn't quite need to be burdened with my Witch's powers, or at least a world where I could embrace the ignorance of an ordinary human. Your despair is tied to mine, and if you continue your duties as a hero . . . forget the sloppy job on your seal . . . we can truly enter the infinite. But for now, enjoy some peaceful days."

"Whoa, baor, Raa!" I yelled in nonsensical frustration. I was being treated like an impatient dog out on a walk, one perhaps bred for cuteness and amusement rather than strength and independence.

With that, the Witch's room dissolved in a storm of cherry blossoms, and I was once again floating in the shifting columns of aether. I felt the wounds I'd sustained begin to heal. My body felt human again, although I knew that deep down, the Diamorph transformations couldn't simply be undone. However, as long as I could pass for normal in the mortal realm, I would have no major complaints. If the biggest thing to worry about was a bad school lunch or a boring Social Studies project, I would do as my patron suggested and enjoy my peaceful days. While part of me wanted to be credited for saving the world, having an adventure unknown to mortals also meant I didn't have to deal with the troubles that came with fame.

"The doll that simulated Abyss will be de-activated and repaired for future use." A computerized female voice said. "Per Dorothy's program . . . beginning transfer in t-minus five seconds. Four, three, two, one . . ."

EPILOGUE

"Didn't get enough sleep last night?" I heard a voice I hadn't heard in over three months. It was one of my closest friends at school, a bespectacled boy named Daigo. "I know that Social Studies can be boring, but come on, Abyss . . ."

Huh? That was the first thing that came to mind. If I recalled correctly, I'd been given that name because I'd suddenly forgotten my previous name.

It was just a name, so why had this also been overridden?

"Was I always called Abyss?" I asked.

"Yeah, it's a weird name," Daigo said. "You said your parents gave it to you back when we first met in sixth grade." I looked at the papers and worksheets on my desk and saw that it was now mid-September, well into my eighth-grade school year. I looked around further, and when I tried to move my right hand, I found that it was still throbbing with pain and was partially wrapped in bandages. "Don't rush when it comes to healing a broken bone, Abyss," Daigo said.

"Did you also see me barf up some silver liquid recently?" I asked.

"Why? Did you try to eat mercury from the thermometer?" Daigo asked. There was, of course, the possibility that my entire adventure had just been an odd dream, and I contemplated on whether or not it was better if I treated it as such, until . . .

"Class, stop working on your reports, and let me introduce our new student," Mr. Dells, our Social Studies teacher, said.

"It appeared that she really had trouble finding her way in the halls. But tardiness will not be tolerated next time, Diana."

Diana looked surprisingly good in modern clothing—instead of the familiar brown tunic decorated with animal pelts, she now wore a simple blue jacket, a light green T-shirt, and a set of baggy jeans. The familiar black markings on her cheeks were still there, however, and she looked in my direction before addressing the crowd. "Hi everyone, sorry I'm late," she said. "I'm Diana Sobekhotep, and I transferred from Easthill Junior High. My interests are mainly track and field and archery. It's nice to meet you all." She definitely didn't pick up on the modern social tact, although it didn't seem like she cared.

"Why are you looking at her like that?" Daigo asked me. "Oh, could you be going through the teenage blues already? First, it was Mitchell and his antics last year, and now you?"

"I . . ." I muttered. "Just thought her cheek tattoos looked interesting." I knew it sounded like a lame excuse, but I couldn't just tell Daigo that I'd gone through an epic adventure and that she'd saved my life multiple times, including dealing the final blow against Krakazrlr because I couldn't properly use that diamond blade. He probably would be somewhat envious or maybe think he could do better, actually.

Even though we were eighth graders, boys still sat with boys, and girls still sat with girls. Still, Diana took a seat that was close enough to keep an eye on me and also for me to keep an eye on her. I noticed that she really hadn't been given any time to mesh into the modern world. "Your handwriting's that bad, Diana?" one of the girls asked.

"Did you come from a foreign country?" another asked.

I could tell that Diana was bored out of her skull by the worksheets and textbooks and probably really regretted having given me For One's Glory. She'd been too used to hunting and gathering when she wasn't helping heroes with their quests, after all. And part of me felt like my brain had adjusted to the grind of combat and physical exertion. Simple things like fill-in-the-blanks and short answers began to elude me when I was conditioned to watch out for sneak attacks and think of my next meal.

My parents would definitely be pretty disappointed if my grades started dropping to Cs . . .

When the lunch bell finally rang, I decided to walk up to Diana and did my best to ignore Daigo and the other students.

"Keeping kids caged up like this is nonsense," Diana grumbled. "And I don't want to have to really learn writing another language. The Pharaoh mostly wanted me to crunch numbers and do some hieroglyphics, but the teachers of your day really know how to assign useless things. And what the hell is with the *spelling* of some of these English words?"

"Well, we might have something good at the school lunch," I said. The cafeteria usually had plain sandwiches and the occasional pizza, although, like most students, I'd brought my lunches from home. "But where are you even sleeping for the nights?" I asked.

"There are a few abandoned warehouses here and there," Diana said. "All it takes to hide me is putting up a magic field." As Diana and I walked out of the classroom and into the hallways, a lot of the other eighth graders turned their attention to us. I'd been known as a nerdy, weird kid for the previous year, and some people on the basketball team still knew me from pick-up games. "I can't believe hundreds of people fit into this one little area, either," Diana added. "Stripping the earth bare so that people can live like ants, huh?"

I sighed.

No matter what, Diana would never be a proper girlfriend. But in that sense, if she freaked people out with her weirdness, at least I wouldn't have to deal with a petty love triangle. "Well, I appreciate you bothering to step out of your comfort zone so that I wouldn't degenerate or whatever after that battle with Krakazrlr. And you saved me with the final arrow at the end, too. I'll try to help you learn reading and writing the best I can. And what I picked up for algebra. The quadratic formula song goes like *negative b . . .*"

"Perhaps I'm the one being petty," Diana suddenly admitted as she continued looking around the school. "As annoying as I find it, this is what the Pharaoh Sobekhotep would want. For the youth to be invested in academic and intellectual pursuits instead of chasing down impala or hunched over in the fields farming."

I remembered the last thing that Krakazrlr had said to me, that I was defending humanity out of a mere habit. Even if I didn't know if it was a good or bad thing, it seemed more proper to leave my species as it was after seeing what weird monsters and magic could do. Still, I genuinely wished that I'd just been tasked with saving a little kingdom from an evil empire. "What made you decide to choose me to handle For One's Glory?" I asked. I realized that she hadn't quite given me a proper answer, and now that I'd met my patron Witch face-to-face, I wanted to feel like I had at least done something right.

"It might have been foolish. It's something I'm supposed to do with most heroes, but I have bad memories of when I tried it." Diana said. "When I used For One's Glory, the best-case scenario was usually the hero degenerating, both physically and mentally, due to my failure to make a proper connection. The worst-case scenario was when heroes . . . turned into villains, like many heroes do, after growing mad with power and becoming desensitized to fighting and killing." It didn't sound like a hopeful future for me, but perhaps Oljatu or the Pharaoh would be happy about that. "I thought that you could properly handle the power," Diana said. "You were reckless, for sure, but at the same time, you did try your best to save me. But regardless of your intents, your fate might be up to the whims of that legendary Witch."

Diana let the subject drop as she waited in the short line in the cafeteria. I lent her some pocket money and sat down at a table with my own boxed lunch. I felt a little bad for not sitting with Daigo and his group like I usually did and wondered if I could drag him into this hero business someday. We had always talked about comics and superheroes and had even tried writing some stories together. I wondered how Simon was faring in his mortal life? And if Latis and Inder were finally relieved that they didn't have to assist such a clumsy hero.

"Even your mediocre sandwiches are pretty good," Diana said as she came back from the cafeteria store. "Bread and spices really do give the meat a new texture. But it's not worth being cooped up in the cage of modern civilization."

"Maybe . . ." I started. "Maybe if we have time outside of school or training or whatever, we could watch a movie or play some video games," I suggested. "Although I'm not sure what my parents would think of you, there are still a few arcades in the inner city."

"Sitting down for over seven hours is already getting my archery skills rusty," Diana said. "You should practice some boxing and swordsmanship, too, especially if the diamond blade calls for you again."

"I suppose I could ask my parents about it, although they'll probably think it's too dangerous. Maybe I've just got to make sure I can snack on some octopus so that it can come in a clutch for me like it did in the coliseum," I said. As if on cue, something pulsed in my chest. It wasn't quite as uncomfortable as the feeling of the quicksilver aether, but Diana was quick to notice.

"Let's do a check-up now," Diana said as she grasped my cheeks.

At first, I thought she might be going in for a kiss, but instead, she inspected my neck as if looking at my esophagus and spine.

"All right, I'll have to do a practice sync, but you should be fine. If you ever feel anything weird, even if it's in the middle of the night, call me over." I wasn't sure if Diana had a smartphone, but it wasn't exactly something I could complain about.

The two of us made our way to an abandoned hallway, and Diana gestured for me to face the wall. "Is something sprouting from my back? I'd like to have at least one of those cool appendages that Krakazrlr got."

"Hold still," Diana said as I felt a sharp sensation pierce the back of my neck. Immediately, I felt raw emotion, as if I was an unruly child, a screeching, wild beast of the jungle. I remembered how the God of Fire stated that humanity had called him to free them from the dull routines of everyday existence. I felt a vulnerable, woozy feeling in my heart, and soon began to realize that these were Diana's experiences and memories. And deep inside, another drive for power and destruction seemed larger than before. I'd thought that I would never have what it took to be the warlord Oljatu desired, but I suddenly remembered the raw power from riding Ibonus and conquering the other tribe.

Weren't these just mere products of evolution, to be compassionate enough to bond, but ruthless enough to conquer?

But the product was usually sealed by restraints, and For One's Glory would produce unlimited . . .

Shlllk.

The greed that had welled up in my heart vanished once more as Diana pulled out the object from the nape of my neck. I turned around and felt a bit embarrassed to be exposed like this. "So was it bad?" I asked.

"For now, it's not," Diana said with vulnerability in her eyes. "Even though I always want to be prepared for the worst, using For One's Glory always brings me back to my old, pathetic self."

"Maybe it's not you," I said. "Maybe it's the heroes who are the pathetic ones for giving up on their ideals so easily." I could see that after this practice sync was done, Diana soon began to revert to her cool exterior.

"It's nothing I haven't heard before," she said. "Even if it's an illusion, I want to feel like I made the right choice by saving you."

Diana got through the rest of the school day still grumbling and bored, and as we left school together, a handful of the other eighth graders continued to stare at us and gossip.

"Abyss going for the new girl. Never thought it'd be the nerdy boy to step up to the plate so soon."

"I think she's pretty cute, even if she's weird. Weird complements weird, right?"

I tried to shrug off those comments, and Diana didn't appear to be bothered either.

"You sure you don't want to grow your hair out now?" I asked. There were a handful of girls with short hair, but Diana hadn't decided to comb it down either. "Maybe you could braid it or something?"

"I'll maybe grow my hair long when you grow a full beard," Diana replied. That likely wouldn't be anytime soon, even if many other boys were growing stubble.

Even though I wanted to fully enjoy the peaceful days I'd been granted, I knew I couldn't simply live life as another young teenager awkwardly transitioning into adolescence. I knew that Dorothy and the God of Fire certainly expected me to perform weirder and crazier stunts in response to my new threats, and in addition, I didn't want to disappoint Diana, Latis, or Inder. And there was so much unfinished business with Oljatu and the Pharaoh, who were both definitely planning things in the shadows.

After school, instead of hanging out in the library or shooting some hoops, Diana and I made our way to an old, abandoned park in the inner city while we looked for affordable gym memberships on my smartphone. I would have to worry about my grades after I put in a good day of training.

While other kids were worried about making a sports team, wearing fashionable makeup, or performing well academically, this four-millennia old tomboy and I were preparing ourselves for our next quest to save the world—whether that was for better or for worse.

"It's still off by a few inches, so I'm recovering as well," Diana said after she had shot three arrows at the target she'd pinned on the tree. I was practicing my left jab and footwork and was still waiting for my injured right arm to heal up.

And so, for a short while, I thought that there would be plenty to look forward to, both in my peaceful days and in my next adventure as a hero. Even if the Witches and monsters watching over me had a limitless supply of weird tricks to play, I felt like I could tackle it as long as Diana was here. I knew that this was only the beginning, and I couldn't help but fall victim to my optimism—regardless of the bumpy start, I believed I would become a proper hero one day. I wouldn't make the mistakes that condemned Captain Drake and his men to wandering the stormy mutagenic seas. And maybe one day, Simon and Justin would see me worthy of retaining my original quest.

Perhaps I'm the one to blame for the following misfortune, but who was I anyway?

I would soon learn that my patron Witch hadn't been merely joking when talking about despair. For every droplet and split second of a happy dream I stumbled upon, the shadows of nightmares continued to fall upon me.

The Pharaoh, the clerics, and the thousands of species that I was borrowing power from weren't eager to let me have significant rest or peace of mind. When I had contracted with the

Witch, I had entered into a bizarre and complex situation that would give the greatest lawyers headaches.

For the boy named Abyss, he could only properly blossom into the meaningless chaos of the beings long abandoned by space and time.

AUTHOR'S NOTES

As a writer, after your first few stories and novels, you begin to learn how many different worlds out there that are really possible—and at the same time, as the years go by, you discover that regardless of talent, no one person can write everything. It's always been an ideal of mine to write high fantasy with vivid details and many characters while keeping the rolling plots with great suspense on, to who can possibly live and die. I knew that in my earlier childhood days, I wasn't always keen on spinning the wheel of tragedy, but throughout over a decade of writing, I didn't question why things had to be so dark.

The best thing about working in a creative field is that when you produce, days don't mindlessly become routine. And that's precisely the worst part of it because, even to the most experienced, there's always room for self-doubt and criticism. Most publishers don't reply with specifics, and it will be pretty difficult to find a large crowd of possible editors. There's always the question of trying to write a work that's flexible enough to appeal to many or trying to write the best overall story and themes. And freak accidents tend to happen—because my first publisher that I published *Generations of Shade* with passed away, I decided to brush off this manuscript and send it out. I never planned to make enough money off of writing alone, even if it was always a dream. But in life, consistent success can become boring quickly, right?

I don't think I'll ever be able to produce the comic relief that many audiences welcome, nor do I find happy endings necessary. That being said, this current story was written in an attempt to gain a larger target audience and to write a more straightforward story that left far less open-ends. I think I would be embarrassed to reduce my work to using the most popular of tropes, and there's always some serious philosophical concern that I want to explore. Why can't monsters just be monsters, and villains just be villains? Well, the real world doesn't produce enough villains for each hero, and would villains really be so generous to go at the heroes one at a time?

Whether it's the classic Diomedes beating up Ares, or 12-year-old Percy Jackson, fighting against a god will always be an intriguing power fantasy. At the same time, I didn't want to write an assortment of monsters that were conveniently dumb enough to be manipulated but smart enough to walk, talk, and follow orders. There are a lot of things that we gain from language and strategy, but there's also a purity in writing the animalistic struggle to hunt and eat. This is never an issue in video games, but humans really do have to eat a lot compared to other animals. It's always a good tradition to have the hero feast after winning a major battle, but perhaps it's an even better experiment to have him half-starving. After all, regardless of your super-power, all the energy used for bending the laws of physics just enough has to come from somewhere, right?

At some point in my writing, I had also given up on using romance as a secondary plot line. It's oftentimes part of the package when it comes to slapping on happy endings. Still, right now, even if I feel like romance doesn't have to be explicit, having the possibility and the character's frustrations always adds some substance. Perhaps it's a sign of laziness, but many shows and web novels can get by with having a harem option. I wanted to make sure that even if Abyss wants to save the weak and unfortunate, there won't always be a girl conveniently waiting to be saved at the end of each level.

At the end of the day, I want to write something that sells, but I also don't want to make consuming my works to be an easy escape. I want to write something that's fun enough to be an adventure, but never insist that if there is the slim possibility that my readers go on a secret mission as a hero that things will be convenient. Still, if Abyss were to be put in a conference room with my other original characters, he would probably feel grateful in comparison to the other possibilities.

Best,

Andy Hsieh

About the Author

Andy Hsieh is a sci-fi and fantasy enthusiast. Although his first passion is creative writing, he also creates animations, illustrations, and independent video games, and is always eager to experiment with and explore new ideas. After starting his initial attempts at writing fiction in middle school, he has retained a strong interest in the stories of antiheroes and villains, peculiar philosophical conundrums and epic quests for adventure. Throughout many trials, tribulations and incomplete projects, he found the determination to push on and improve through many years of raw experience. Hsieh graduated with his B.A. in Philosophy, Law and Society in 2017, and currently resides in Northern California.

www.ingramcontent.com/pod-product-compliance
Lightning Source LLC
LaVergne TN
LVHW020634100826
845148LV00012B/2182

* 9 7 8 1 4 8 7 4 4 1 2 0 3 *